Gérard de Villiers

LORD OF THE SWALLOWS

Gérard de Villiers (1929–2013) is the most popular writer of spy thrillers in French history. His two-hundred-odd books about the adventures of the Austrian nobleman and freelance CIA operative Malko Linge have sold millions of copies.

Malko Linge, who first appeared in 1965, has often been compared to Ian Fleming's hero James Bond. The two secret agents share a taste for gunplay and kinky sex, but de Villiers was a journalist at heart, and his books are based on constant travel and reporting in dozens of countries.

On several occasions de Villiers was even ahead of the news. His 1980 novel has Islamists killing President Anwar el-Sādāt of Egypt a year before the event took place. *Revenge of the Kremlin* suggests Vladimir Putin ordered the assassination of an exiled Russian oligarch in 2013. *Lord of the Swallows* is based on the 2010 discovery of a network of KGB spies living undercover for decades in the United States ("swallow" is Russian slang for a sleeper espionage agent).

ALSO BY GÉRARD DE VILLIERS

The Madmen of Benghazi
Chaos in Kabul
Revenge of the Kremlin

LORD
OF THE
SWALLOWS

LORD

OF THE

SWALLOWS

A MALKO LINGE NOVEL

Gérard de Villiers

Translated from the French by William Rodarmor

Vintage Crime/Black Lizard

Vintage Books

A Division of Penguin Random House LLC | New York

A VINTAGE CRIME/BLACK LIZARD ORIGINAL, FEBRUARY 2016

Translation copyright © 2016 by William Rodarmor

All rights reserved. Published in the United States by Vintage Books,
a division of Penguin Random House LLC, New York, and in Canada by
Random House of Canada, a division of Penguin Random House Ltd.,
Toronto. Originally published in France as *Le maître des hirondelles* by
Éditions Gérard de Villiers, Paris, in 2011. Copyright © 2011
by Éditions Gérard de Villiers.

Vintage is a registered trademark and Vintage Crime/Black Lizard and
colophon are trademarks of Penguin Random House LLC.

The Library of Congress Cataloging-in-Publication Data
Villiers, Gérard de, 1929–2013.
[Maître des hirondelles. English]
Lord of the swallows : a Malko Linge novel / by Gérard de Villiers ;
translated from the French by William Rodarmor.
pages cm. — (Vintage Crime/Black Lizard)
1. Spy stories.   2. Suspense fiction.   I. Rodarmor, William, translator.
II. Title.
PQ2682.I44 M3513 2015   843'.914—dc23   2015020374

Vintage Books Trade Paperback ISBN: 978-0-8041-6937-0
eBook ISBN: 978-0-8041-6938-7

Book design by Joy O'Meara

www.weeklylizard.com

Printed in the United States of America
10 9 8 7 6 5 4 3 2 1

LORD

OF THE

SWALLOWS

CHAPTER 1

Monte Carlo, Monaco

For maybe the tenth time, the blonde at the end of the banquet table gave Malko the eye.

Intriguing.

When she caught him looking back, a discreet smile lit up her face, revealing small, gleaming white teeth. But then her tablemate said something to her, and she turned her head to answer him.

Malko continued watching her. The woman was clearly interested in him. But she wasn't alone. Her companion was a tall, gray-haired man with a strong, set face behind steel-rimmed glasses. A Protestant banker type.

Though no great beauty, the blonde was more appealing than her partner. She had a pert nose, regular features, and light blue eyes emphasized by her careful makeup. Small breasts swelled the décolletage of a well-cut ball gown. When she and her companion first sat down, Malko had noticed another thing about her: an unusually attractive ass. It was probably her best physical attribute, because her face and hair weren't especially notable.

She was now looking insistently at him again, with the same slight smile. She was clearly trying to catch his eye.

But Malko knew that Alexandra was watching him as well. His longtime fiancée was seated farther down the table, and he quickly flashed her a loving, complicit smile. Countess Alexandra Vogel was a tigress who always slept with one eye open, and there was no point in provoking her. It was a good thing the unknown blonde didn't have the kind of body to arouse her intense jealousy. Alexandra herself wasn't totally faithful to Malko, but any female drawn to his golden eyes became a potential murder victim.

Actually, he wouldn't even have noticed the blonde if she hadn't been sending him those flirtatious glances.

Just then, Malko's friend and host Helmut Ponickau gave him a cheerful wave from his seat, which was nearest the dance floor. Onstage above him, the vintage crooner Tom Jones was trying to liven up the stolid guests at this Red Cross Ball, a major event on the Monte Carlo social calendar.

Baron Ponickau had invited Malko and Alexandra to the fund-raising gala, along with three other couples, Italian and American. Malko found this kind of event deadly dull, but he couldn't very well refuse, because the baron often invited him to sumptuous hunts and elegant parties at his castle in Upper Austria.

A charming man with impeccable manners, Ponickau was wellborn, rich, and as snobbish as a royal gynecologist. With the help of carefully chosen intermediaries, he had managed to obtain Monaco residency, which saved him a lot in taxes and probably explained his fondness for the principality. Malko, on the other hand, thought Monaco looked like the stage set for an operetta. It was dwarfed by skyscrapers and riddled with tunnels, its stately old pastel-colored buildings gradually being buried under new concrete.

He found himself wondering if Ponickau's invitation had been an indirect way for the baron to spend time with the alluring Alexandra. In Vienna, it was rumored that she and the baron had had an affair during one of Malko's many trips abroad for the CIA. Was it true? Malko was hardly blameless when it came to fidelity, so he never raised the question. Resolving that kind of ambiguity usually comes at a cost.

Now increasingly intrigued, Malko glanced at the blonde again. She didn't look like a seductress. He tried to remember at least her first name from when they were introduced, but in vain. Ponickau had met his guests at the entrance of the Sporting d'Été de Monte-Carlo at the end of Princess Grace Avenue, near the principality's border. They gathered in the marble hall that led to both the Privé casino and the Salle des Étoiles, where the Red Cross gala was held. Introductions were made quickly, and Malko hadn't remembered anybody's name. That hardly mattered. Except for the baron, he would probably never see any of these people again.

Now he was in a hurry to get back to the Hôtel de Paris for an intimate tête-à-tête with Alexandra, who looked dazzling in a cobalt blue sheath cut high on her left thigh.

Tom Jones finished his set, and a modest round of applause echoed through the ballroom.

Malko discreetly glanced at his Breitling; the evening's torture would soon be over.

It had started with dinner, a display of pretentious neo-classic cuisine that had lasted the full two hours it took to serve the three hundred guests. This was followed by the inevitable fund-raising auction, where blasé millionaires pretended to fight over the jewelry put up for bid by the evening's sponsors.

The winners would then bestow the jewels on their mistresses or their housekeepers.

Thank God it was for a good cause.

Of which causes there were no shortages. The floods in Pakistan had displaced the Haiti earthquake and the Darfur massacres, which were already losing some of their cachet.

The highlight of the evening was yet to come, however: the opening of the ball by His Most Serene Highness Prince Albert II. The Prince of Monaco was escorting the tall, muscular South African swimmer he was engaged to marry.

As the orchestra was setting up, Baron Ponickau kept his eyes fixed on the adjoining table. He had discreetly slipped the Sporting concierge five thousand euros for the signal honor of being seated at the table next to Prince Albert. That way he would be one of the first people to reach the dance floor after the prince and, naturally, be photographed there.

It was a modest reward for the fifteen thousand euros the baron had paid for his table, but in the eyes of the Monégasques, proximity to the princely family was a key that opened every door.

In the ballroom, the long tables were arranged banquet style. They each had ten place settings and stretched to the back of the room.

The orchestra began playing the first notes of what was probably a waltz, and the hall held its collective breath as the prince stood up and reached out to his fiancée.

Malko gazed at the starry sky above them, revealed by the retractable roof of the well-named Salle des Étoiles.

Prince Albert and his swimmer were now whirling gracefully to the rhythm of an old-fashioned waltz.

Ponickau promptly stood up, adjusted his beautifully cut tuxedo, and—to Malko's surprise—extended his hand to Alexandra, who was seated opposite him.

She had no choice but to accept. Malko watched her get up and felt a pang when she pressed her gorgeous body against the baron's. His wife, Hildegard, carried fifty pounds of extra ballast, and could hardly compete.

At that point, everyone hurried onto the dance floor. Aside from the social lepers at the back tables and some doddering graybeards, everybody wanted to rub elbows with His Most Serene Highness. In an instant, the only two people left sitting at Ponickau's table were Malko and the mysterious blonde.

Clearly feeling abandoned, she gave Malko a look so imploring, it would have melted stone.

Within moments, they were spinning around the dance floor as well. Even in four-inch heels, she was so much smaller than Malko that her blond head rested against the lapel of his tuxedo. After a few waltz steps, she looked up at him and asked:

"Are you a friend of Helmut's?" Her voice was high and a bit grating.

"I am indeed. Are you?"

"He's mainly friends with my husband. We often have him to our house when he comes to New York. He's a charming man."

"Are you American?"

She spoke perfect English but with a slight accent.

"I have an American passport, but I'm Russian. I left the Soviet Union in 1991 to come to New York. I worked as a nanny and a sales clerk before meeting my husband, Tim Bartok."

"Is that the man you're with, this evening?"

"No," she said. "That's my second husband, Alexei Khrenkov. He's Russian too. He's in finance."

"So you've kept your first name—Zhanna," concluded Malko, who had glanced at her place card on their way to the dance floor.

"That's right. Please tell me about yourself."

"I'm Austrian."

"I already knew that," she said teasingly. "Helmut told me about you. You live in a beautiful castle, I hear."

"Beautiful. . . . That's saying a lot."

The orchestra briefly paused, but Zhanna stayed in Malko's arms until it resumed, playing a piece that mixed salsa and reggae. Malko had the impression that his partner's hips were drawing closer to his. In any case, there were now so many dancers on the floor that he probably could have pulled Zhanna's panties down without anybody noticing.

"What are you doing after the ball?" she asked.

The older guests were already beginning to slip away. In a few minutes Prince Albert would do the same.

"I'm planning to go back to my hotel."

"Aren't you going to the casino?"

"No, I don't gamble."

"Just like my husband!" she cried. "I love to gamble. I think I'll try my favorite number at the Privé before going to bed. My husband seems very taken by his neighbor, that Italian who claims to be a princess. Would you mind coming to the casino with me for a few minutes? I hate going to places like that by myself."

This time, her gambit was unmistakable. Their eyes met, and, as if to back up her request, the young woman briefly pressed her hips against his.

Zhanna Khrenkov didn't appeal to him that much, so he was only slightly stirred by the move.

"I think my fiancée will want to go back soon," he said.

"Are you sure?" Zhanna said with a mocking smile. "She seems to be having a very good time."

And in fact, Alexandra was dancing the salsa/reggae in slow time, her body glued to Ponickau's.

"Leave her to her fun," Zhanna insisted as they returned to their table. "We won't be gone long."

Malko was trapped.

So he made his way through the dancers and set a light but possessive hand on Alexandra's rump. Over the sound of the music, he said:

"Our friend Zhanna asked me to go to the Privé for a few moments. Want to come along?"

Alexandra's refusal was chilly, and Malko didn't insist. Zhanna was standing at the edge of the dance floor, purse in hand.

They had only to cross the narrow Sporting d'Été hall to reach the Privé, where they showed their identification. Because Monaco followed French law, you had to show ID before being allowed into a casino. Zhanna pulled out a blue American passport, and Malko presented his purple Austrian one.

Entering the casino, he was surprised to find the room nearly empty. Half the roulette and blackjack tables were already covered in green baize.

A gambling hell-hole, it wasn't.

Zhanna came back from the cage with a handful of chips.

"Come on!" she cried gaily.

In the next room, which was somewhat livelier, she went to the roulette table and slapped two five-hundred-euro chips firmly on number 24.

"There! I hope you bring me luck!"

Alas, that wasn't the case.

The croupier raked off Zhanna's bets five times in a row. With a resigned sigh, she put her last two chips on 24 again.

Miraculously, after bouncing around a little, the ivory ball came to rest on 24.

"*Harasho!*" she cried in the classic Russian phrase as she briskly scooped the seventy-six chips into her purse.

"Let me buy you a glass of champagne," she said, making her way to the bar. "You really did bring me luck. I usually never win."

But when the bartender reached for an open bottle of champagne, she stopped him.

"No, I want a fresh bottle!" To Malko, she said, "What do you recommend?"

"Taittinger Comtes de Champagne Rosé 2004," he told the bartender while stealing an anxious glance at his watch. They had left the Salle des Étoiles twenty minutes earlier, and Alexandra was probably fit to be tied—for no good reason!

The Taittinger cork gave a joyous *pop!* and he and Zhanna toasted each other.

"*Nasdarovie!*" he said.

"You speak Russian?"

"*Da, kanyeshna,*" he said with a smile.

"I like you more and more," she purred, sipping her champagne.

"I don't want to keep your husband waiting," he said cautiously.

"*Davai,* then!" she cried, leaving a five-hundred-euro chip on the counter.

Their table in the Salle des Étoiles was now practically empty, as was the rest of the ballroom. Of their party, only the American couple and the two Italians remained.

"Helmut left with his wife and Prince Linge's friend," said the American. "He took Alexei along, too."

Malko frowned. Alexandra must be in a rage, he thought. But Zhanna gave him no time to say anything.

"Where are you staying?" she asked.

"At the Hôtel de Paris."

"So am I."

"I'll call us a taxi."

"Don't bother," she said. "Our car must still be in the lot, since Alexei went with Helmut. I'll drive us back."

Malko didn't argue. After saying good-bye to the two other couples, he and Zhanna headed for the Italian restaurant that led to Jimmy'z, the famous Monte Carlo nightclub with a garage on the heliport for the club's patrons.

The parking valet came running the moment he spotted Zhanna.

"I'll bring your car right away, Madame Khrenkov!"

"Where is it parked?"

"On the right over there, just beyond the hedge."

"Give me the keys. I'll get it myself."

Bowing so low he was practically spread-eagled, the valet yelped with joy when Zhanna gave him a five-hundred-euro chip in exchange for the car keys.

Malko followed her across the open space and past the low hedge along a VIP parking area filled with Rolls-Royces, Lamborghinis, Ferraris, and a lone Bugatti. Zhanna got into a gray Bentley coupe.

Malko climbed in as well, but Zhanna didn't start the engine. She gave him a meaningful look and quietly said:

"I very much enjoyed meeting you."

"The pleasure was mutual."

Smiling enigmatically, she suddenly brought her face close to his.

Only a boor would be so rude as to not at least give the young woman a good-night kiss, a quick peck without any romantic implications. Their lips touched chastely for an instant, but then the young Russian started kissing Malko in earnest, her little tongue probing for his. At the same time she grasped the nape of his neck, as if to keep him from pulling back, and the kiss became deeper. It was a real movie kiss, like the one Grace Kelly shared with her lover in *Dial M for Murder*.

This burst of apparently sincere passion aroused Malko's libido. Alexandra's going to be angry anyway, he thought, so she may as well have a reason for it.

But when he put his hand on Zhanna's thigh, she pulled away, breathless.

"I find you enormously attractive," she said, her eyes shining.

The kiss seemed the logical extension of their flirtatious glances over dinner.

The Bentley's engine purred to life and Zhanna switched on the headlights. She drove out onto Princess Grace Avenue. There was still a lot of traffic, and they moved at a snail's pace.

Without looking at Malko, she abruptly said:

"I'd like to see you again."

This was an unexpected development. Malko glanced at her out of the corner of his eye. Zhanna's public persona was proper and self-effacing; she was no sex kitten. Still waters run deep, he thought.

Malko hadn't moved when she spoke again, quietly.

"Don't get too close to me. I think we're being followed."

Malko's pulse speeded up.

"By who?"

"My husband is very jealous."

Leonid Androsov drove the rental Mercedes carefully and cautiously. A veteran of Russia's elite Alpha counterterrorism unit, he could do just about anything, from garroting a man to dismantling a diesel engine. Androsov had been parked at a bus stop outside the Sporting d'Été, and started following the Bentley when it emerged. His inconspicuous black Mercedes was no different from the dozens of others driving around Monaco, and the Bentley's Swiss license plate was easy to make out in the darkness.

Seated next to Androsov, Grigory Lissenko was chewing on an unlit cigarillo and taking notes for their daily report. Their team watched the Khrenkovs in eight-hour shifts, like in a factory. This required twelve men, because the couple didn't always travel together.

Twenty minutes later, the Hôtel de Paris finally came into view.

The Bentley pulled into the hotel's valet parking area, which was full of luxury vehicles. Crowds of modestly dressed sightseers slipped in among them to take one another's pictures, happily posing next to Rolls-Royces and Ferraris, under the vaguely contemptuous gaze of the hotel security people.

A gorgeous brunette in a bright red ultra-short skirt slowly made her way across the restricted parking lot and headed for the casino. For her, the hour of the hunt had arrived. But competition among the call girls was fierce. The Moldovans, for example, were facing a wave of aggressive women from the Baltic, who were even taller and more beautiful.

The Bentley stopped in front of the hotel, and a valet parker rushed over to open the door.

Zhanna turned to Malko with an ambiguous smile. They hadn't made a move toward each other since their passionate kiss in the parking lot.

"What's your room number?" she asked.

"It's 406, but—"

"You're not alone, I know. Neither am I. And as I said, my husband keeps an eye on me. But I want to see you again."

"That seems pretty difficult," said Malko, who wasn't too

motivated. The somewhat ordinary blonde didn't especially turn him on.

"We'll manage!" she said. "Give me your cell number."

After a brief hesitation, Malko gave her his number, and she keyed it into her iPhone.

"I'll see you soon!" she said.

They got out together and climbed the steps to the hotel. Zhanna hadn't given him her room number, he noted.

That was cautious of her.

The center of the lobby was occupied by a huge table bearing a ten-foot-high flower arrangement. As they walked around it, Malko was still unsure why this seemingly well-behaved woman had come on to him. And something else intrigued him: despite the passion of her kiss, he had the feeling Zhanna was playing a role.

But what role, and why?

Lissenko stepped out of the Mercedes, which then reversed out of the hotel lot and went to park down the avenue. He smoothly climbed the hotel steps. A martial artist and former wrestler, he was all muscle. He could easily kill a man with his bare hands, and had often done so.

He had developed a specialty in Chechnya, where he was given captured *boiviki* guerillas to execute. He would lock his muscular thighs around the man's chest, seize his head in his huge hands, and violently twist it. Cervical vertebrae shattered, the prisoner died without a sound.

Inside the hotel, Lissenko spotted the tall Austrian he was tailing. The man was standing to the left of the monumental staircase leading up to the boutiques, waiting for one of the elevators. Lissenko strolled over to the elevator, and when the cabin arrived, he quickly stepped in. His "target" had already pushed the button for the fourth floor, so he pushed number three and waited, studying the tips of his loafers.

He was completely calm.

Lissenko no longer felt any emotion when on a mission, and this one was especially easy. He probably had forty pounds on his neighbor in the elevator, and could strangle him with one hand.

Without looking at the other man, Lissenko stepped out of the elevator at the third floor onto an elegantly appointed landing with an authentic Louis XV desk. Moving quickly, he made for the stairwell and climbed a flight, stopping with his head level with the fourth floor. Hearing the elevator stop, he watched through the crack under the stairwell door as the man turned left and passed by without seeing him. Lissenko climbed the remaining steps, slipped silently through the doorway, and followed him down the narrow hallway leading to the Rotonde wing of the hotel. On the plush blue carpet, the Russian moved without a sound.

CHAPTER

2

Reaching Room 406, Malko slid his key card in the lock and opened the door. At a glance, he could tell the suite was empty, and his pulse ticked up a notch. Where was Alexandra?

Her cell phone and purse lay on the bed, so she had stopped by the room and must be somewhere in the hotel, but where—and with whom?

Malko left the room and headed back down the twisting hallway, his footsteps muffled by the blue carpet. Just before he reached the elevator landing, he noticed a husky man walking ahead of him.

Even from the back, Malko recognized the stranger who'd gotten off the elevator on the third floor. What was he doing here?

When they reached the landing, the man got into the elevator without turning around, leaving Malko to wonder about him.

One thing was clear: the man had been following him but had been surprised when he came back out of the room. Who could he be?

Malko immediately thought back to the car that had followed Zhanna's Bentley when they came out of the Sporting d'Été. Bodyguards on her jealous husband's payroll, she'd said.

Malko promised himself to steer clear of her. She wasn't attractive enough to be worth risking trouble. And right now, he had to find Alexandra. If she wasn't with a man in one of the Hôtel de Paris's hundreds of rooms, she could only be at the bar.

Alain Ducasse's restaurant Le Louis XV was closed, and it wouldn't be like Alexandra to waste her time in the shopping gallery. Malko quickly scanned the lobby, whose vast marble floor made it feel almost like a cathedral. A dozen gorgeous Eastern European women sat along a table on the left, on the lookout for clients entering the hotel alone.

Their eyes lit up when Malko passed, but he ignored them and stepped into the Bar Américain, where a band was playing an insipid jazz tune. There weren't many customers, but Malko's heart skipped a beat when he spotted Alexandra's cobalt blue dress in the back of the room.

His fiancée was sitting with the Ponickaus and Zhanna's husband around a bottle of Taittinger champagne in a crystal ice bucket.

There was no sign of Zhanna.

Alexandra greeted Malko with an ironic sally.

"So, did you win?"

"I didn't gamble," he said. "Isn't Zhanna with you? We came back together a few minutes ago."

"She must have gone to bed," said Khrenkov. "Did she come out ahead, at least? I'm surprised she wanted to gamble. She hates casinos."

Though he didn't let it show, Malko was surprised. The outgoing Russian blonde had fooled him. The only reason for her sudden urge to play her favorite number was to be alone with him. Zhanna's newfound passion was assuming unexpected proportions.

Khrenkov finished his glass of champagne and stood up.

"Good night, everyone," he said. "I'm going to bed. I'm sure Zhanna is already asleep."

Alexandra crossed her legs with deliberate slowness, looked Helmut Ponickau in the eye, and said:

"I'd like to go dancing someplace less depressing than the Sporting."

"We could go to Jimmy'z," the baron suggested.

Malko, who had a terrific urge to get Alexandra into bed, promptly scotched the nascent plan.

"It's barely one in the morning," he said. "Nobody shows up there before two."

Alexandra recrossed her long legs, briefly flashing white satin panties.

"Too bad," she said.

Seeing Malko's look of annoyance, Ponickau declared a truce.

"We'll go some other time!" he said. "I'm feeling a bit tired, too. Let's just finish the champagne."

He took the bottle and poured the rest of the Taittinger into their glasses.

They all wound up in front of the elevators together, but they separated on the fourth floor: the Ponickaus were staying in another wing of the hotel. Walking to Room 406, Alexandra tripped on the carpet. When Malko caught her and put his arm around her waist, she whirled on him, hissing like an angry cat.

"Didn't you enjoy the blow job?"

Malko kept his cool.

"Don't talk nonsense," he said. "The woman doesn't do a thing for me. You're the one I want."

She shrugged and pulled free.

"Her husband looks like an undertaker, so I understand why she might want some distraction. You think I didn't see what she was up to, during the whole dinner? She couldn't take her eyes off you. If she could have gotten to you under the table, she would've done it."

"Well, Helmut couldn't take his eyes off you, either," he retorted.

"Helmut has always liked me," she said with a nasty smile. "I thought you knew. In fact, if he weren't with his fat cow of a wife, I think he would've asked me up to his room."

"And you would have gone?"

"I like being desired. And he has a lot of charm."

"Have you two been lovers?"

Malko was putting the key card in the door lock.

"Curiosity is an ugly fault," she said, stubbornly turning away from him.

Standing slightly akimbo, Alexandra gave Malko a challenging look, and he felt his desire for her catch fire. The moment they were inside, he shoved her against the wall and slipped his hand through the slit in her skirt to her upper thigh.

"I can't tell if Helmut wanted to make love to you tonight," he said, "but I'm going to be the one to do it."

Alexandra didn't stir, even when he started to rub her through the satin panties.

"She couldn't have given you much of a blow job," she said coolly. "I'm not surprised. She looks more like a businesswoman than a slut."

He shoved the panties aside and forced his way into Alexandra's most intimate parts, going as deep as he could.

"You're hurting me," she said coldly. "People usually handle me more gently."

She was openly defying him.

He angrily grabbed the panties and yanked them down her slim, tapered thighs.

"I don't feel like making love," she said.

"Neither do I," he snapped. "I just want you to suck me off, the way you do so well."

Her defiant attitude was inflaming his libido, already aroused by the brief interlude with Zhanna Khrenkov. Feeling his cock swell, Malko rubbed gently against Alexandra, who continued to pretend not to notice. When he pulled himself out of his trousers, she lowered her eyes, feigning indifference.

"Do you really want to?"

Without answering, he seized her neck and pulled her head toward him. When she resisted, he pushed down on her shoulders, forcing her to kneel.

The hard part was done.

In surrender, Alexandra took the stiffening cock in her mouth. Her natural sensuality aroused, she began to give Malko what he'd demanded.

Eyes closed, he leaned back against the wall. Alexandra's unfair accusation had sparked a fantasy: he now imagined that it was Zhanna, with her lively little tongue, who was sucking his prick. He twisted Alexandra's long blond hair into a knot, and used it to push even deeper into his unresisting fiancée's mouth.

He came with a groan of pleasure.

She was still the best.

But when he opened his eyes, he found Alexandra looking at him strangely.

"If I said you were the second man to come in my mouth this evening, would you believe me?"

Without waiting for an answer, she snatched up her panties and went to the bathroom, locking the door.

Malko felt as if he'd been stabbed in the heart. Alexandra was quite capable of doing what she claimed, just to get back at him. He could remember some of the outlandish places where the two of them had made love in the past. The Hôtel de Paris had enough nooks and crannies to shelter a quickie.

Malko started to take off his tuxedo, promising himself to never see the Russian blonde again.

The Khrenkovs were eating breakfast in the sitting room of their suite.

"It would be nice to invite our friends to Ducasse's place before we leave," Zhanna suggested, breaking the silence.

"Sure," agreed her husband distractedly as he read the emails on his iPhone.

"I'll invite the Linges, too," she said casually.

At that, Khrenkov quit reading and shot her a look of annoyance.

"Do you really want to? Those aren't people we should be seeing, and you know it."

Zhanna was unmoved.

"There's no risk," she said firmly.

Khrenkov gave her a long, searching look.

"I'm not an idiot, Zhanna. I know you find him attractive. You should be more careful."

She didn't bother answering, merely stood up and said:

"I'm going down to the spa. I'll drop off the invitations at the front desk."

The moment she left, Khrenkov traded his iPhone for a small, very heavy cell phone. This was the secure, bug-proof telephone he used to communicate with his security detail. When he had its chief on the line, he gave him his instructions. Vladimir Krazovsky's team wasn't directly under his command, but they took orders from him. They also filed reports on all his requests.

Feeling reassured, Khrenkov turned his attention back to the

Tokyo stock market. Zhanna is being reckless, he thought. Surprising, for such a strong woman. Or else she wants revenge.

When Khrenkov phoned, Krazovsky was in the Méridien dining room, eating a hearty, Russian-style breakfast with one of his men, Gleb Yurchenko.

Except for the night shift, who were resting, the other team members were at nearby tables. More Russian was spoken in the restaurant than French or English these days. The Méridien Beach Hotel was also the Eastern call girls' base of operations. The women had noticed the Russian security team but asked no questions. They saw them as neutral, neither threats nor customers. They figured the men probably worked for a Monaco security service for visiting oligarchs. Back in Russia, having bodyguards was a status symbol, even if you didn't need them.

The team leader hung up and relayed Khrenkov's orders to Yurchenko.

"We're leaving in ten minutes," he said. "We'll go to the casino parking garage." This was an underground lot across from the Sporting d'Hiver and the Hôtel de Paris. The security guards didn't get to use valet parking unless the job required it.

Krazovsky then went looking for Grigory Lissenko, to find out what he had learned about the target the previous evening.

The mood around the lunch table was falsely cordial.

The phony Italian princess and her husband had left for Rome. The Khrenkovs' American friends were dazzled by Le Louis XV's sumptuous décor. Across the way stood the Monte Carlo Casino, designed by Charles Garnier. Crowds of sightseers on the Place du

Casino gazed up at the rich people on the wide restaurant terrace, hoping to spot celebrities.

Helmut Ponickau was keeping the conversation going, helped by Zhanna and one of her American girlfriends.

Sitting as stiff as a statue of the commander, Alexandra was icy. She stared at the horizon, as if hoping a dragon would swoop down and swallow Zhanna in one bite. For her part, Zhanna glanced often at Malko but more discreetly than the previous evening. She was wearing a very sexy outfit: an almost transparent top and linen pants so tight they seemed painted on.

Fortunately, they had reached dessert, a delicious raspberry soufflé, cooked by Ducasse himself, that had the Americans drooling.

Over coffee, they started exchanging business cards to stay in touch. Malko and Ponickau didn't need each other's cards, of course, but Malko handed cards with his Liezen Castle address to the two American couples.

Clearly showing her irritation, Alexandra didn't exchange cards with anyone, and the air-kisses that followed were chilly. The party split up in the lobby.

"I'm going to do some shopping," Alexandra announced. She didn't invite Malko along, which was unusual. The others headed for the elevators.

Malko hadn't been in his room for more than ten minutes when the phone rang. Probably Alexandra, he thought. She's feeling guilty.

It was Zhanna.

"I'm downstairs in the spa," she said in her somewhat harsh voice. "Alexei has gone to the bank, and will be there for a while. We could have a drink together."

Malko nearly hung up on her. After a long silence, the Russian woman continued, sounding seductive:

"I absolutely must see you before you leave."

There was more than sexiness in her tone, and Malko was intrigued.

"Why?"

"I'll tell you in person. It's important."

She hung up without waiting for his answer.

After a long hesitation, Malko put on a jogging outfit and a white terry-cloth robe. Something told him that libido wasn't the only reason Zhanna wanted to see him.

CHAPTER

3

A small elevator led directly to the spa on the ground floor. It had a view of the harbor and included an indoor pool, fitness and massage rooms, and a sauna. It also had a snack bar, whose only customer was Zhanna Khrenkov.

Seeing Malko, she brightened.

"I knew you would come!"

"How did you know?" he asked, sitting down.

"Because you're not afraid of jealous husbands," she said.

"Do you cheat on him often?" he asked sharply.

"Never. Besides, what makes you think I want to cheat with you?"

She really is a cool customer, thought Malko, remembering the scene in the Bentley and the young Russian woman's tongue diving for his tonsils.

As if she could tell what he was thinking, she smiled and said:

"I know, I behaved like a teenager in heat. It was because of your strange golden eyes. It was a kind of fantasy, but it isn't going any further."

"In that case, why did you want to see me?"

"You're a fascinating man. And right now I need somebody like you."

"To do what?"

"I can't tell you yet. I don't have much time."

"Then I don't see how I can help you. As my friends the Ponickaus probably told you, I'm just a country squire who lives quietly in a castle in Austria."

"They told me many good things about you. You're a very romantic character."

"Thank you," said Malko, looking at his watch. "I'm going to join Alexandra in her shopping now. You and I probably won't see each other again."

A cloud crossed her face.

"If that were the case, I would be very disappointed," she said. "I will be in London next month, and my husband is going to New York for a few weeks. I'd like to see you there."

"I don't live in London."

"There are flights from Vienna."

Zhanna had gotten to her feet. She gave him a searching look.

"If you come, you won't regret it," she said quietly.

Malko merely bowed, kissed her hand lightly, and headed for the door. He was determined to never again see this odd woman.

He took the only exit from the spa, a little hallway leading to the elevator. When he reached it, two people appeared behind him: burly guys in white T-shirts and pants, built like weight lifters.

Probably masseurs, he thought.

They politely stepped aside to let Malko into the small elevator cabin, which barely had room for the three of them. Suddenly one of the men turned and faced him. When Malko met his eye, he immediately understood he was no masseur. Before he had time to wonder further, the stranger viciously head-butted him.

Luckily, the man was a good six inches taller than Malko, so the blow landed between his eyes instead of breaking his nose. Malko groggily fell against the second "masseur," who elbowed him in the ribs so hard he almost threw up.

Now bent over, he took a punch in the stomach that felt like a battering ram, and this time he vomited bile on his attacker's crisp white T-shirt. The man jerked back, growling furiously. Then a muscular forearm clamped a headlock around Malko's throat. He felt himself being lifted off the ground as the pressure on his carotid arteries increased.

He dimly realized that he was going to die in the little elevator without even knowing why.

After a few seconds, the pressure eased enough for Malko to gulp some air, but his relief was short. He screamed, feeling something sharp jab a quarter inch into his left side: a knife.

The man facing Malko leaned close enough to touch his face, and asked:

"*Vui gavarite po russki?*"

Malko nodded that yes, he spoke Russian. The man continued in that language:

"If you don't want to die, never approach Zhanna Khrenkov again. Understand?"

Malko gulped and said, "*Da.*"

The man backed away and pulled the knife out. Then a hand ran down his body, and huge fingers grabbed his balls, crushing them.

"Never, got it?" the man said.

Malko thought he was going to throw up again.

Then the man pressed his thumbs on Malko's carotids. In seconds, he felt the blood leaving his head and passed out, slumping heavily to the elevator floor. He vaguely felt the second man stepping over him, then nothing.

A woman's screams finally brought Malko back to consciousness.

Opening his eyes, he saw sandals, a pair of sunburned calves, and the hem of a blue dress. Then the panicky face of a fat woman who was awkwardly trying to help him up.

"Are you all right?" She spoke French with a strong British accent. "You must call a doctor."

Bracing himself against the elevator wall, Malko managed to get to his feet and force a smile.

"I'm okay," he assured her in English. "I just got dizzy. The heat, you know."

He stumbled out of the cabin, which was still at the spa level, and the elevator went up with the British woman on board. Leaning against the wall so as not to collapse, Malko felt he'd been put through the wringer.

It was unreal: he'd been savagely attacked in the most stylish hotel in Monte Carlo! Though truth be told, security wasn't the Hôtel de Paris's strong suit. Guests were checked as they came in through the main revolving doors, but after that, nothing. Anybody could go upstairs to the rooms, and there were very few security cameras.

Malko pressed the elevator button and glanced down at the spreading bloodstain on his shirt. The attack had been no dream.

He began to feel better only when he got to his room. Alexandra hadn't returned, which was just as well. Malko tore off his clothes and ran to the bathroom for a long shower.

The hot water did him good.

Then he bandaged the wound and stretched out on the bed.

He cursed Zhanna Khrenkov, who knew full well how jealous her husband was. But he wasn't especially surprised by the treatment he'd gotten. It was typical Russian brutality. The men who beat him up were professionals: military veterans turned bodyguards, used to killing first and asking questions later.

One thing mystified him, however. They seemed to know that

he spoke Russian, whereas only Zhanna was aware of that. Who could have tipped them off?

Malko hadn't answered the question before drifting off to sleep.

This time, Malko invited the Ponickaus to dinner at the Rampoldi, the famed Italian restaurant up the street from the casino. Alexandra, who hadn't noticed anything unusual, was very much at ease. Also, she was delighted with her latest purchase: a tight, uniform-style dress with officer epaulets and a neckline that flirted with indecency. Teetering on six-inch heels, she was taller than any of them.

Helmut Ponickau couldn't take his eyes off Alexandra's tanned breasts, and he wound up spilling half his basil spaghetti on the tablecloth.

Which tended to reinforce Malko's suspicions. Maybe Alexandra actually did have two men come in her mouth the evening before.

"Let's have a drink at the Hôtel de Paris bar," suggested Ponickau, who was in no hurry to lose her, especially as the bar was within walking distance.

They had barely been shown to a table when the two women got up and went to the bathroom. Malko took advantage of their absence to ask:

"Helmut, have you told your Russian friends much about me?"

Ponickau gave a small, satisfied laugh.

"Of course. I told them how much I liked you."

"Is that all?"

The Austrian baron leaned close, looking mysterious.

"I told them that nobody knows where you get the money you're spending on your castle."

"They must think I'm a crook."

"Oh, no! I said a lot of people in Vienna think you're a spy, that you work for the CIA. It's an open secret, isn't it?"

Before Malko could answer, the two women returned, and the men stood up for them.

With its dark woodwork and wide windows, the ambassador's private dining room was pleasantly luxurious. The embassy was located on Boltzmanngasse, and Vienna's famous Prater Ferris wheel could be seen in the distance.

Sitting at the table, Matt Hopkins grinned as happily as a schoolboy playing hooky.

"We're lucky to be able to get in here," said the Vienna CIA station chief to Malko. "The ambassador is a stickler for the rules. When he goes out of town, he locks his dining room. But His Excellency is in Washington all this week, and I'm friendly with his secretary."

A Marine waiter took their drinks order the moment they sat down. Malko asked for vodka; his CIA colleague, Chivas on the rocks. They waited for the waiter to serve their drinks and a gazpacho appetizer before discussing anything serious.

"Did you come to Vienna by yourself?" asked Hopkins.

"No, Alexandra is with me. She's out shopping. Then she'll go home for the grape harvest."

"You'll have to introduce me to the countess sometime," said Hopkins with a somewhat dreamy smile. "I've been told she's very beautiful."

The station chief had clearly been hearing about Malko's voluptuous fiancée.

"Next time, Matt. I promise."

As Hopkins finished his gazpacho, Malko said:

"So tell me, have you found out anything interesting about my two Russian friends?"

"You bet! They're crooks, both of them. Big-time crooks."

Hopkins pulled a file sheet from his pocket and summarized its contents. Born in 1962, Alexei Khrenkov was a brilliant graduate of the Moscow Institute of Finance and Economics. At age twenty-eight he went to work for Inkombank and soon became its president. In 1998 the bank started to collapse, and angry American stockholders discovered they'd been relieved of sixty million dollars.

"But Alexei goes on to bigger and better things," said Hopkins.

In spite of his shady past, he became minister of finance for the Moscow region in March 2000. Four years later, he became vice minister of the Moscow Oblast, handling all real estate transactions and public contracting.

"This is where our boy really shows what he can do," said Hopkins. "It's also when his wife comes into the picture. This is Zhanna, formerly Bartok. After spending a few years in the United States, she returns to Russia and meets Alexei. They fall madly in love."

They also become accomplices.

Advised by her husband, Zhanna Khrenkov set up a series of shell companies to process orders from the Moscow region, submitting invoices inflated by 40 to 75 percent. The scammed money was deposited in their offshore accounts.

"Meanwhile, Zhanna travels back and forth to the United States," continued Hopkins. "Thanks to the money embezzled from the Moscow Oblast, she makes a splash in New York. She buys a residence on East Eighty-Third Street off Park Avenue and becomes a boldface name through her charity work. She brings the Russian National Orchestra to town and organizes a 'Russia' show at the Guggenheim Museum and in Miami.

"Zhanna also treats herself to a few trinkets," he went on. "An investigation by the Moscow FSB's financial section found that she spent twenty-six thousand dollars on shoes and lingerie in just one month in 2003."

"Now there's a woman who knows how to live!" exclaimed Malko sarcastically.

"At Inkombank's expense, in those days," said Hopkins. "But that was peanuts, compared to what comes next. Between 2004 and 2008, the two manage to skim twenty-seven billion rubles from the Moscow region; that was about seven hundred million dollars at the time. In 2008, they feel the wind shifting, and they quietly leave Russia and go abroad, dividing their time between New York, London, and the French Riviera."

"So what did the Russian authorities do?" asked Malko.

"The Moscow FSB and the MVD both filed lawsuits against them, but no international arrest warrant was issued."

"That's a bit strange, isn't it?"

"Our sources in Moscow say that Alexei Khrenkov has long been protected by General Boris Gromov, the commander of Soviet troops in Afghanistan until 1989. He was probably on the take as well."

Just then, the waiter brought in lamb chops and broccoli and poured them an excellent Château La Lagune 1994.

"It's a typical Russian story," said Malko after the man left.

"So where did you run into our two friends?" Hopkins asked.

"At the Red Cross Ball in Monte Carlo, this summer."

"Quite a step up for a forty-three-year-old Belarusian school-teacher!" said Hopkins with a smile. "Why did you get interested in them?"

Malko saw no reason not to satisfy the station chief's curiosity.

"It started with an innocent flirtation at the dinner," he explained. "And it almost ended up very badly for me."

Hopkins listened to the story of the elevator attack in fascination.

"Well, that completes the picture!" he said when Malko finished. "Not only is Zhanna Khrenkov a crook, she's also cheating on her husband. I'll add that to her file."

"What do you make of the incident in the elevator?"

"Pretty much what I'd expect," said Hopkins. "A guy like Khrenkov will have bodyguards, and you know the Russians aren't given to subtlety."

"That's true, but I still don't understand why this woman came on to me so strongly."

The American burst out laughing.

"Malko! Everybody knows that you're a born seducer. Zhanna's probably bored, for all her money. She wanted to have a fling."

"It still seems odd," said Malko, shaking his head. "She just isn't the type. She's a cold fish, and doesn't have any special charm."

"You're being too modest. What other reason could she have?"

"I don't know," Malko admitted. "But her persistence surprised me. The last time we talked, she asked me to come see her in London, where she has an apartment. She spoke of some mysterious reason that she would tell me about later."

"That's normal enough. She's following through."

"But she has a husband who keeps an eye on her."

Hopkins grinned again.

"Here's what I find interesting, Malko. I get the sense that you want to see her again. And mind you, I can't provide Agency protection in that case. It's strictly private business. So try not to get yourself roughed up too badly."

Malko smiled without answering, and they talked about other things until the coffee came.

Privately, he had to admit that the CIA station chief was right.

Was Zhanna drawn to him because Helmut had hinted that he worked in intelligence? Or did the two crooked Russians have some twisted plan to use him?

He glanced at his Breitling. Alexandra would be getting impatient.

"I'll be heading back to Liezen later," he said. "You'll have to come visit sometime. It will give you a chance to meet Alexandra."

A delighted Hopkins walked him out to the embassy courtyard, where Malko's butler/bodyguard, Elko Krisantem, was waiting at the wheel of the Jaguar.

Alexandra was sitting in the Rote Café, wearing a print dress Malko had never seen before. It was tight and revealing in all the right places, the way she liked it. Malko sat down and put his hand on her thigh.

"You're looking very sexy!"

"That's exactly what one of your friends said a moment ago," she said with a teasing smile. "So what did those spooks of yours have to say?"

Alexandra hated Malko's parallel existence, but she recognized that he needed the CIA assignments to support his lifestyle—and hers.

"There might be a little something in London. Making a contact. You like London, don't you?"

Alexandra frowned.

"You know perfectly well that I can't leave the vineyard now. The fermentations are complete, and I have to do the tastings, not to mention keeping an eye on the pruning. I probably shouldn't even have come to Vienna today. Anyway, I'd like some champagne before we head back to the country."

Within minutes they were toasting each other with Taittinger Brut.

"Ah, that's better," she said with a contented sigh. "Champagne really is a wonderful drink."

A little later, as they were driving to Liezen, Malko wondered why he had lied to her. It was far from clear that he would be seeing Zhanna Khrenkov, or even that he wanted to.

His id had spoken in his stead.

While Alexandra was changing, Malko went into the library to read, and Krisantem brought him the day's mail on a tray. A large envelope with a British stamp caught Malko's eye, and he opened it first.

Printed on gold embossed stationery, it was an invitation from the ambassador of Kazakhstan to Great Britain to an evening at Christie's the following week for a gala honoring Kazakh art.

Turning the invitation over, Malko saw a large red mark on the back: it was a kiss, in bright scarlet lipstick.

```
┌─ CHAPTER ─┐

    4

└           ┘
```

Only one person would have sent him such a suggestive invitation: Zhanna Khrenkov.

She certainly didn't give up easily, Malko reflected.

Hearing the click of high heels on the marble entry to the library, he quickly hid the invitation between two books. Alexandra walked in wearing a short, tight dress with enough uplift to cheer a depressive.

"We're going to be late!" she cried. "Their damned castle is way out in the sticks!"

Malko followed Alexandra down the hall, watching her rump sway like a sexual metronome. But he was so preoccupied by the London invitation that he forgot to caress his fiancée while driving, as he usually did.

His dilemma was simple: go to London or not?

The gala was a week away, and beyond a few social calls, Malko had nothing special on his calendar. Alexandra was busy with the vineyard and couldn't accompany him, so that was no problem. But how should he respond to Zhanna's invitation?

In spite of her passionate come-on in Monaco, he felt no special attraction for the blond Belarusian.

But as they neared their evening's destination, Malko had to admit that the situation intrigued him. Now that he knew

Zhanna's history, he suspected that her insistence on seeing him hid something more complicated than an affair.

Climbing the steps of their hosts' home, Malko made up his mind: he was going to London.

Sitting with a cup of tea in front of the windows of her Grosvenor Place penthouse, Zhanna distractedly contemplated Buckingham Palace's impeccable grounds with more than a touch of satisfaction. At number 18, her flat was next to the Irish embassy on Grosvenor Place, which ran along Buckingham Park in Belgravia, the most fashionable neighborhood in London.

What a long road it had been from her communal apartment in Minsk and the pathetic salary she earned in the days of the Soviet Union! Just escaping from Belorussia and moving to Moscow was a big step, even though she'd been forced to work as a *domorabotnitsa*—a housemaid—to survive in the Russian capital.

She would never have dreamed that the Queen of England would someday be her next-door neighbor.

Alexei had left for Bern an hour earlier. He would then travel to New York to deal with an urgent problem that had come up. The Russian authorities had frozen one of their bank accounts, which held twenty-three million dollars.

Zhanna didn't usually spend much time in London, but she decided to stay behind. A man of few words, Alexei made no comment, but she was wary of his apparent indifference. He took a few of the bodyguards along; the rest stayed behind in London, supposedly to protect her.

In theory, the men were at her beck and call, but she didn't control their movements and didn't trust them. They took their orders from Moscow, and she had no power to intervene. In a way, they were the price of her and Alexei's freedom.

On paper, her "guardian angels" worked for an import company called Petropavlovsk, and all had proper visas.

The men were stationed not far from the penthouse and could come in minutes if Zhanna needed them. But she suspected them of sticking their noses into her private life, checking her mail and even her phone calls.

Alexei's impromptu trip gave her the idea of inviting Prince Malko Linge to take her husband's place at the Christie's gala. She was one of the evening's sponsors, so making the switch was easy. To her, the funniest part was that the evening was being indirectly paid for by the Russian taxpayers.

Zhanna lit a cigarette and gazed at the trees in the palace gardens.

Would Malko reply to her invitation?

On its landing approach, the British Airways flight banked low over the forests west of London. Malko hadn't been back to London since an unpleasant run-in with the Mossad a year before. He hoped the Israelis no longer bore him a grudge.

Busy with her vineyard affairs, Alexandra hadn't said anything when he announced his brief trip to London. She didn't know that the Khrenkovs had a residence there, so she had no reason to be suspicious.

Malko had decided not to contact the London CIA station or even to mention his trip to Matt Hopkins in Vienna. His curiosity about Zhanna didn't involve the CIA, and probably never would. But while riding in a taxi to the Lanesborough, Malko felt annoyed with himself. He was behaving like a high schooler. Accepting an invitation from a woman he didn't desire, and who had already caused him pain, was pure masochism.

At the gala, Malko would probably learn Zhanna's real intentions. British MI5 would probably note his presence in London but realize it was for personal reasons.

Looking elegant in a gray bowler and pink boutonniere, the Lanesborough porter greeted Malko by name, as if he had left only the night before.

Taxis were pulling up one after another at 10 King Street, a one-way alley between Piccadilly and Pall Mall lined with art galleries and one old pub, the Golden Lion.

Malko's cab was followed by a Rolls-Royce with an odd license plate, consisting of just three letters. A heavyset couple got out. The man's head was shaved; the woman was a dark, chubby gypsy type, with a low forehead and slightly slanted eyes.

A throng of tuxedos and ball gowns hurried into Christie's, clustering at a long table bearing place cards with table assignments for the Khrenkovs' two hundred guests.

Malko looked around for Zhanna but didn't see her. Many people had already climbed the monumental stairs to the first floor, where cocktails were being served. After getting a place card assigning him to Table 8, Malko followed suit.

Battalions of waiters made their way among the guests, carrying trays of champagne and soft drinks. Kazakhstan was officially a Muslim country, but forty years of Soviet occupation had reduced the role of religion in the wealthy desert nation, and the Islam practiced there was soft as well.

Malko tried to take an interest in the paintings on the walls, but most of them were dreck, Soviet realism at its worst: naïve, assembly-line knockoffs of the sort littering the Izmaylovo Market in Moscow.

Christie's is a venerable, serious auction house, thought Malko, so the evening's sponsors must have paid a pretty penny to persuade it to display paintings that were worth less than their frames.

After cruising through the crowd a few times, Malko had to face facts: Zhanna wasn't there. There were few attractive women aside from the handful of Russian, Ukrainian, or Moldovan prostitutes who had married well. Almost everyone was speaking Russian or Kazakh.

The crowd fairly reeked of prosperity. Malko overheard a conversation between two bankers, one of whom whispered:

"I've already spotted a dozen millionaires, including four Kazakhs."

For a brand-new country, even a very big one, that was encouraging.

Malko was on his third glass of champagne when dinner was announced. He followed the crowd into a dining room with midnight blue walls and a very high, octagonal ceiling.

Table 8 was in the back facing the door, next to a stage presumably set up for musicians. The couple from the Rolls-Royce was already seated and greeted Malko with friendly smiles. They were joined by a man with strongly Asian features accompanied by a curvaceous blonde twenty years his junior. They were Russian as well.

A tall young woman wearing a turban sat down at Malko's right. She had a lean face and an air of class. In Russian-accented English, she asked him:

"Are you interested in Kazakh art?"

"Only very slightly," he admitted. "What about you?"

"I run a gallery in Moscow, and we tend more to the contemporary. The foreign market for Kazakh art is minuscule. These works are mainly bought by Kazakhs."

"I hope they don't pay too much for them," said Malko, studying the nearest painting. It showed a couple in the field of a 1930 collective farm, their faces as expressive as gargoyles'.

The gallery owner merely smiled politely. No point in ruffling potential customers.

Nearly everyone was seated now, but an empty chair remained at Malko's left. Leaning over, he read the guest's name on the card: *Lynn Marsh.*

Maybe this was Zhanna Khrenkov, under another name.

A stocky man picked up a microphone and delivered a long speech in Russian that was translated into English, praising Kazakh art, Christie's hospitality, and the wonderful quality of the guests. Mid-speech, Malko saw a woman making her way among the tables toward him. A tall, beautiful brunette in a scarlet sheath dress. She had a striking face, with high cheekbones and a slightly upturned nose.

To Malko's delight, she slipped into the seat next to his. Up close, Lynn Marsh was even lovelier, with a slender figure and a decent neckline. She flashed him a dazzling smile.

"I'm so sorry to be late," she said. "I couldn't get a taxi."

It had been a rough day for London transit: an unusual Tube strike had snarled the city's traffic.

What was odd was that she was apologizing to Malko as if she had a date with him.

The speech over, the toasts began, and their table burst into cheerful cross talk. It now seated four very attractive women, including Lynn. She turned to him and asked:

"Are you in banking?"

"No, why do you ask?"

She laughed.

"There are nothing but bankers here tonight, rich Russians and Kazakhs. Since you're neither Kazakh nor Russian . . ."

"I'm Austrian, and an art lover," he said. "That's why Christie's invited me."

He couldn't very well admit the invitation came from a woman who had come on to him and then stood him up.

"What about you?" he asked. "Are you a banker?"

"No, I'm a dentist."

"Well, you're the most beautiful dentist I've ever seen. I'm sorry I don't have any trouble with my teeth."

"You're lucky!" she said, laughing merrily. "I'm very expensive."

Her own teeth were perfect.

At this point, everyone at their table was speaking Russian except the two of them. Malko continued in English.

"Did Christie's invite you as well?"

Lynn shook her head.

"No, I was supposed to come with a Russian friend, but he had to go on a trip. I enjoy getting dressed up. It's a nice change from dentistry."

One of the covey of waiters set a plate of something in front of Malko. The menu called it foie gras, but when Malko tasted it, he was pretty sure the pâté had ridden from Kazakhstan on horseback, maybe even wearing the saddle. Catching Lynn's eye, he gave her a complicit smile.

"The foie gras is a bit odd, don't you think?"

The Russians and Kazakhs nearby were gleefully stuffing themselves with it.

Malko again scanned the room, looking for Zhanna.

There was no sign of her.

He glanced over at his tablemate, who was ignoring her tasteless foie gras and typing on her iPhone. She looked preoccupied.

She's gorgeous and outgoing, thought Malko. What an amazing coincidence that the most beautiful single woman at the dinner should be seated next to me!

CHAPTER

5

The foie gras was followed by an interminable musical interlude: two singers with tambourines performing Kazakh songs. A mix of fast rhythmic tempos not unlike Moroccan music, it suggested riders galloping across Kazakhstan's famously oil-rich steppes. It brought tears to the eyes of the Kazakh couple at Malko's table.

After a roar of applause, dinner resumed with a main course that made Malko wary. The only edible things he could identify were some green beans huddled next to a chunk of mystery meat, but his Kazakh tablemates cleaned their plates.

This was followed by yet another speech.

Malko was mystified: Why hadn't Zhanna shown up? Fortunately, Lynn Marsh was happy to chat. Among other things, he learned that she was divorced.

As the evening drew to a close, he was no further along. He gallantly fetched Lynn a plate of macaroons from the dessert table in the next room. She was charming, though she kept glancing at her watch. By the time she finished her macaroons, nearly all the guests had left.

"I think we better get going!" she said brightly, standing up, purse in hand.

They walked down the monumental staircase side by side and

stepped out into the icy wind sweeping down King Street. Fortunately, taxis regularly turned in from Duke Street, and several arrived one after another.

Lynn looked ravishing in her long red dress. Malko figured he didn't have much time if he wanted to end the evening on a more intimate note.

But she beat him to the punch.

"I'm so happy to have met you!" she cried, giving him her dazzling smile. "This turned out to be a wonderful evening. Fate works in mysterious ways."

They were standing on the narrow sidewalk opposite Christie's.

"Would you like to have a drink at Annabel's?" he asked.

"I'm sorry, but no," she said with an apologetic smile. "I have to get up very early to be at my office by eight. Another time, though."

During dinner, Lynn had given Malko her card with her phone number. He found it odd that such a beautiful woman should be slaving away in a dental office. He hadn't dared ask who had invited her to the gala. If it was her lover, it was surprising that he hadn't shown up.

In the face of the young woman's determination, he merely smiled and kissed her hand.

"Another time, then," he said.

Malko followed her with his eyes as she walked toward a taxi.

Regarding Zhanna's inexplicable absence, he had moved from being baffled to angry and disappointed. What had gone wrong?

There was nothing left but to head back to the Lanesborough.

No doubt about it, he thought. Women just can't be trusted.

Zhanna Khrenkov slipped out of the Leicester Square Theatre before the end of the performance. Protected from the cold wind by her fur-lined Burberry, she walked to Piccadilly Circus and took a taxi. She figured there was little chance of her being followed.

At the Lanesborough, she crossed the lobby to the small lounge next to the bar and ordered an herbal tea. At this late hour, it was empty.

Zhanna didn't know what time the Christie's gala would end. From her perch she could see everybody who entered the hotel lobby.

She waited more than twenty minutes, growing increasingly impatient. She knew that Malko was staying here at the Lanesborough; she had phoned earlier to check, giving a made-up name. Of course it was possible that he wouldn't come straight back to the hotel.

Finally she saw a man in a tuxedo and topcoat enter the lobby and head for the elevators. It was Malko! She immediately got up and went to stand behind him. Opening the gilded elevator door, he sensed her presence and turned around.

"Zhanna! Where have you been?"

"I'll explain in a moment," she said with a playful smile.

She had already stepped into the cabin, which meant she intended to go directly to his room. Malko closed the door and pushed the button for the second floor.

When they got to his room, she turned and slowly opened her Burberry, revealing a short pink lace dress and shiny black stockings. She was perched on a pair of Jimmy Choos, whose heels were studded with fake diamonds. Eyes underlined with mascara and a red mouth completed the picture.

Shedding the Burberry, she looked at Malko, a hand on her hip.

"So, do you regret coming to London?"

"Why weren't you at Christie's?"

"Something came up. But I'm here now."

Her nipples were straining against the pink lace, and Malko could tell she wasn't wearing a bra.

Joining deed to words, Zhanna came over and stood close, moving her hips suggestively. Then she raised her face to his and said simply:

"Kiss me."

He did. It was as abrupt as in Monte Carlo.

Reaching behind her back, she unzipped her dress and stepped out of it. Underneath she was wearing a very elegant black-and-mauve slip. Combined with the Jimmy Choos, it made quite a sophisticated picture.

Zhanna twirled around.

"Do you like it?"

From what he'd learned in Vienna, Malko already knew that she loved lingerie. Without waiting for his answer, she came close again and started stroking him through his alpaca trousers.

In moments, she had settled Malko in a Queen Anne armchair and pulled out his cock. Kneeling on the thick carpet, she took him in her mouth and began giving him a blow job worthy of a professional.

Malko soon felt himself losing control. He wanted to pull free so they could fuck, but Zhanna gripped his cock like a drowning man clinging to a life jacket. Moments later, he came in her mouth.

It was all so strange! Here was a woman dressed to the nines who had dragged a man she supposedly wanted from the depths of Europe, yet she wouldn't make love with him.

Zhanna stood up, straightened her stockings, and gave Malko a look of amusement.

"Is there anything to drink here?"

In the minibar, Malko found a half bottle of Taittinger Brut.

Without putting her dress back on, Zhanna sat down in his armchair and lit a cigarette.

After they toasted each other, Malko gave her a sharp look.

"Why did you want me to come to London, Zhanna?"

"Aren't you feeling satisfied?" she asked with a teasing pout. "Didn't I show you a good time?"

"Yes, of course."

Zhanna was acting less like a woman in love than a professional pleased to have satisfied a good customer. Her fellatio had been perfectly executed, but without a speck of eroticism. It was like an after-dinner mint, served expertly and mechanically.

She set down her champagne glass.

"Did you like your tablemate?" she asked, as if she could tell what else was on Malko's mind. "Dr. Marsh is a very pretty woman, isn't she? Did she try to pick you up?"

Malko stared at her in astonishment.

"How do you know who was sitting beside me?"

"I drew up the plan for the table, and I put you next to her," she said simply. "A good choice, don't you think? Only she must have been disappointed."

"Why?"

"Because Alexei should have been sitting in your seat."

"Alexei Khrenkov, your husband?"

"Who is also her lover."

Things were getting more and more confusing. But Malko glimpsed one possibility: Zhanna had invited him to the gala so he could seduce her husband's mistress. It was pretty twisted. But during the dinner Lynn Marsh hadn't given any signal that she was available.

"Please explain," he said. "You want me to seduce this woman?"

Zhanna's carefully made-up mouth twisted into a sneer.

"Not really," she said. "I'd like you to get rid of her for me."

The moment Lynn got home, she grabbed her cell and phoned Alexei. She knew about his unplanned trip, but he had suggested she go to the gala anyway, for fun.

Now she missed him badly and wanted to talk. And it wasn't yet seven o'clock in New York.

Finally, her lover came on the line.

"Are you back at your flat?" he asked.

"Yes. I missed you terribly."

"I was going to call," he said. "I was afraid you wouldn't be home yet."

"Why wouldn't I be?"

"Weren't there any unattached men at the party? Starting with whoever took my seat?"

"Oh yes!" she exclaimed. "A charming gentleman. He's an Austrian prince, an art lover."

The silence that followed was so long that she eventually asked if he was still there.

"Yes, yes, I'm here."

"Are you coming home soon?"

"In a few days."

"I want you back in London. I want you to make love to me," she said.

The two of them had met by chance. Khrenkov's original dental appointment was with Lynn's better-known office mate, but he was out sick that day. When Khrenkov came to the office, she found him very attractive, in spite of his gray hair, Trotsky-ite glasses, and serious mien. A reserved, virile man, he had a hungry look that seemed to cut right through her white lab coat.

Despite their age difference, she accepted his invitation to dinner. She was divorced and didn't have anyone in her life. They went out three days later and made love afterward. Lynn was surprised to discover that Khrenkov had the energy of a man of twenty. Now, months later, their passion hadn't flagged.

"I'll let you go now," he said. "I have a meeting with my lawyer. I'll call you tomorrow."

"Come home soon!"

Having hung up, Khrenkov spent a long moment lost in thought.

An Austrian prince at the Christie's gala! That couldn't be a coincidence. How had Malko Linge gotten there? Only one person could have made it happen: Zhanna, who hated Lynn Marsh. What game was she playing?

And what was Linge up to? Khrenkov remembered what they had learned about him. Lynn might not know anything about the Austrian prince's real life, but the mere fact that he'd met her was a serious threat.

Zhanna is playing with fire, he thought. This wasn't like her. She must really be crazy jealous, because she also knew Linge was a CIA agent.

Khrenkov was now even more in a hurry to get back to London so he could take the necessary measures.

Zhanna coolly put her dress back on, as if her sexual offensive had only been playacting. Having asked Malko to get rid of Lynn Marsh for her, she lit a cigarette while waiting for an answer.

"Do you want me to become her lover?" asked Malko. "Because that would depend on her, and I didn't feel she was available."

Zhanna blew out a puff of smoke and shook her head.

"What I'm asking isn't so complicated. I want you to get rid of her physically."

Malko didn't seem to understand, so she added slowly, stressing the individual words:

"I want you to kill her."

At first Malko thought he hadn't heard right. From mysterious, things had turned gothic. This woman, whom he'd encountered just once in his life and with whom he had no particular connection, was asking him to kill her husband's mistress. Yet she seemed perfectly at ease and clearly wasn't joking.

"Do you think I'm a killer for hire?" he asked, keeping his tone light. "Are you going to offer me money?"

"No," she said. "Something much more valuable."

"But why would I do such a thing?"

"Because it wouldn't be the first time you killed someone."

She was looking at him so intently, he realized that she meant what she said.

"What in the world makes you say that?" he asked, making an effort to sound calm.

Zhanna stubbed out her cigarette in the ashtray.

"I imagine you've killed quite a few people during your missions for the CIA," she said calmly. "Spilling blood doesn't scare you."

Malko managed an almost natural-looking smile. He hadn't been expecting such a direct assault.

"My friend Helmut has been sharing his fantasies, I see."

Zhanna's venomous smile immediately told him that this line of defense wouldn't cut it.

"Don't treat me like an idiot," she said sharply. "I have other sources besides Helmut. Does the name Leonid Shebarshin mean anything to you?"

Of course it did. Shebarshin had headed the KGB's First Chief Directorate from 1989 to 1991.

When Malko didn't answer, Zhanna continued.

"I know you killed a woman named Valentina Starichnaya in the bar of this very hotel."

This time, Malko had to struggle not to show his surprise. Zhanna had brought him back to three years earlier, to 2006, when an FSB hit team had murdered Alexander Litvinenko. The Starichnaya woman had tried to kill Malko and he'd had to shoot her. As if to drive the point home, Zhanna continued:

"I also know that Valentina Starichnaya was acting under orders from Boris Tavetnoy, the deputy head of the London *rezidentura*. Need any more details?"

"No, I don't," said Malko, feeling rattled. "So what do you want?"

There was no point in trying to bluff the woman, he realized. Ponickau couldn't have told her any of this; he didn't know it. Malko was clearly dealing with an extremely well-informed person with links to Russian intelligence.

Zhanna lit another cigarette.

"I've already told you," she said. "I want you to get rid of Lynn Marsh. I don't care if you strangle her, shoot her, poison her, or blow her up. I just don't want her breathing the same air as me anymore."

"Why do you hate her so much?"

"Because that bitch is stealing my husband."

"It's not as if you're completely faithful to him," Malko couldn't help remarking. "You wanted to meet me here on business. You didn't have to make me think it was for an affair."

The Russian woman smiled.

"I felt like it. The bastard is cheating on me, and I wanted to pay him back in kind. But don't get me wrong. I've known Alexei for seventeen years. We've done a lot together, and I still love him."

"You also helped him steal twenty-seven billion rubles from the Moscow oblast."

Zhanna let that pass without comment. Instead, she said:

"He's been acting crazy since meeting the Marsh woman," she continued. "Before that, women didn't matter to him. Now, he's lost his head. All he thinks about is fucking her. To do that in peace, he'll have to get rid of me sooner or later."

"He can get a divorce."

"No, there's too much between us. The only way he'll ever have the perfect romance is by killing me."

A thin smile lit up Zhanna's pale face.

"So from my point of view, it's self-defense."

A position that hadn't occurred to Malko.

"Zhanna, I'm flattered that you thought of me for this operation," he said. "But I've never killed anyone just because I'd been ordered to. Besides, this business is between you and Lynn Marsh. It should be easy for you to farm the job out to someone. The two goons who beat me up in Monte Carlo would do just fine."

"They don't take their orders from me," she said. "I need help from the outside."

Abruptly Malko decided he'd heard enough. He stood up and made for the door.

"Sorry, Zhanna, but I'm not your man. The world has no shortage of hired killers."

The Russian woman didn't stir.

"Do you think I'm a complete fool?" she said. "I never imagined asking you to do this for free."

"I'm not for sale," he said flatly. "Not even for your seven hundred million dollars."

"I'm not trying to buy you!" she protested. "I want to offer you a deal. A deal that will certainly interest your bosses at the CIA. I'm not asking you to be personally involved. The Agency has vast clandestine means. For them, liquidating a person like Lynn Marsh is no problem."

Malko was astounded at her chutzpah.

"Why would the CIA do that?"

"Because it's in their interest. I wanted us to meet so you can transmit an offer they won't be able to turn down."

Malko sensed that this was more than empty talk.

"What's that?"

"There is a network of sleeper Russian spies operating in the United States that the FBI or CIA has never detected because it has no connection with the SVR"—the Russian foreign intelligence service. "Even the Washington and New York *rezidenturas* don't know about it."

"That's nonsense! The Cold War is over."

"But the confrontation between Russia and the United States isn't. You're in a good position to know. Remember the 2008 war in Georgia? If the Americans had uncovered the Russian network operating in Tbilisi, there wouldn't have been an invasion.

"Russia absolutely has to know what American leaders are really thinking. To identify the ones who can be corrupted. We also need a lot of technology. Nowadays, turning a scientist is much more important than persuading some general to defect."

Malko was listening now. It was true that the shadow war was continuing, albeit in a lower key. The operations he'd recently carried out proved it. Zhanna Khrenkov knew what she was talking about.

"All right, let's assume this sleeper network exists," he said. "What's the connection between that and killing Lynn Marsh?"

"There isn't any, except through my proposal. You and your friends get rid of her, and I'll give you the network. Which is working perfectly, by the way. The American agencies can't detect it. The agents have a direct link with only two people: Alexei and me."

Zhanna was seated on the edge of her armchair, leaning slightly forward and speaking deliberately.

Aside from their conversation, silence reigned. The room was hung with curtains, and thick walls muffled any outside noise. The Lanesborough was asleep at this late hour anyway. Even the hookers in the bar had gone home to bed.

Zhanna looked intently at Malko.

"Do you believe me?"

"I don't know. What I've learned about you makes me extremely cautious. I'm sure you honestly want to get rid of your husband's girlfriend, but I have my doubts about the rest. I know how careful the Russian secret services are. Why would they use people like you?"

An ironic smile appeared on Zhanna's pale face.

"You're referring to our problems with the Moscow authorities, aren't you? It's true, we can't set foot in Russia without winding up in Lefortovo, and then Siberia. The MVD is after us, and they've arrested several of our friends, the ones who took a chance and stayed. The Moscow FSB financial section also has a file on us.

"The Americans know all this, and consider us thieves—but anti-Russian thieves! What better cover could we have? Not even the most paranoid CIA analyst would imagine that we work with the Kremlin."

"The Kremlin?" Malko was surprised.

"That's right. The network was set up on the Kremlin's direct initiative, outside of all the official intelligence structures. By people who are aware that the struggle between Russia and the United States is continuing. In the unlikely event the network is uncovered, no SVR agent would be implicated.

"You know Russia well. So you know that in the days of the Soviet Union, the KGB sent waves of sleeper agents abroad. We call them *lastochkas*, 'swallows.' These swallows would have no connection with their superiors for very long periods of time, until they had worked their way into the right positions. At which point they were taken in hand again."

Zhanna paused, and smiled slightly.

"You could call Alexei the lord of the swallows."

Malko's mind was racing. What Zhanna was telling him was certainly plausible. The Russians were masters of intelligence, and he could easily imagine them creating a clandestine network that the official authorities could later disavow.

But one part of the story didn't fit.

"You and Alexei embezzled millions of dollars from the Moscow oblast. Why would they trust you?"

Zhanna burst out laughing.

"Because we're rich! We'd never betray them for money. We're not like most defectors. Or people like Aldrich Ames."

There again, she was right. Most Soviet defectors had done it for the money.

To drive her point home, Zhanna continued:

"You know that the FSB and the MVD are after us for a huge swindle. Don't you find it odd that an international warrant has never been issued for our arrest?"

"Why hasn't it?"

Her smile broadened.

"Because if it were, we wouldn't be able to travel freely and live in the United States. I'm fine. Thanks to my first marriage, I have an American passport, so I can't be deported. But Alexei still uses his Russian passport. And by the way, if we agree on a deal, I'd like him to have an American passport too."

"There's no deal so far," he said, "and I doubt there ever will be."

Zhanna merely shrugged.

"Very well, so be it. Our swallows will continue feathering their nests."

She was putting on her Burberry when Malko asked:

"Assuming your story is true, how did the Kremlin first contact you?"

"Alexei didn't act alone. He had a *krisha*. His protector was a retired general with ties to the Kremlin. He knew we were in trouble, and he suggested we cut a deal and leave the country. The oblast people were planning to send killers after us, and we knew they'd succeed eventually. So we agreed to run the network."

"You were forced to leave Russia in 2008, but this network was in place long before that. Your story doesn't hold water."

Zhanna was unruffled.

"Actually it was created in 1996. The problem was that the head of the network died of cancer in 2007."

"Who was that?"

She gave him a mocking glance.

"Oh, stop treating me like an idiot! The swallows flew free for more than a year but they needed a guide, a führer, as you might say. Alexei fit the bill perfectly."

Malko found this all so startling, he didn't know what to think. There was such an imbalance between eliminating a romantic rival and betraying a spy network that he had trouble believing it.

"Let's get this straight," he said. "You're telling me that to get rid of Lynn Marsh you're ready to deliver an entire network working for your country."

Zhanna smiled ironically.

"First of all, my country is Belarus. I've never been involved in Russian politics. Second, nothing would make me happier than attending that bitch's funeral. If some people have to do jail time for the killing, so be it. At least the death penalty doesn't exist in Great Britain for that kind of crime anymore."

She looked at her watch.

"I have to go now," she said. "They think I've been at the theater. If you want to contact me again, be extremely careful. As I said, our personal security is handled by people who answer to Moscow. They vet all our contacts to make sure no 'pollution' comes close to us.

"If those people got even a whiff of a collusion with you, they wouldn't hesitate to liquidate us. They take their orders from the Kremlin, and they report back regularly."

"How did you figure out who I was?" asked Malko.

"Through them. When we visit people or go out to dinner with someone, they check them out. In your case, it was easy."

Apparently.

Anticipating Malko's next question, Zhanna said:

"It was standard procedure. The Kremlin didn't view your presence as dangerous. Otherwise we would've canceled the dinner."

"What about the attack on me, then?"

"That was Alexei. He wanted to get you away from us for a reason no one would question: jealousy."

Zhanna already had her hand on the door handle when she said:

"To contact me, leave word at the Dorchester Spa. I go there every day when I'm in London. I'll call back on your cell. But pass my offer along quickly. If I'm not going to do business with you, I need to find someone else. I just can't stand to have that bitch having sex with my husband."

She closed the door.

Now alone, Malko wondered if he hadn't been dreaming. The mystery of Zhanna's invitation to London had been cleared up, only to be replaced by another, much bigger one. Either this was an exceptionally clever setup by the Russians, who were experts at this sort of thing, or it was a real chance to roll up a spy network.

What Malko found striking was the disproportionate stakes: a girlfriend versus a network. Only a jealous woman could imagine such a project. Especially since if the people running the network learned of her role, Zhanna wouldn't long outlive her rival.

But one thing was clear: it was up to the CIA to decide what to do next.

The Russians were likely to be particularly ferocious in defending their flock of swallows.

A fascinated Richard Spicer listened to Malko's account of his meeting with Zhanna Khrenkov the night before. When Malko phoned, the CIA station chief had immediately invited him to lunch. Time was short, so they met at the Millennium Hotel on Grosvenor Square, a stone's throw from the American embassy, where the CIA was housed.

They were talking in low voices in a quiet corner of the dining room, surrounded by graying, preoccupied businessmen.

Spicer had taken out a little pad and was taking notes. He looked up when Malko finished.

"At first blush, it sounds like a fairy tale!" he exclaimed. "But I'm not a Russian specialist, so I'll send your account to the Russia desk at the DI"—the Directorate of Intelligence. "Because it's such an unusual approach, I'll also run it by Ted Boteler in special operations. Do you think the feeler is genuine?"

"A lot of what Mrs. Khrenkov told me is accurate," said Malko, who was working on his second espresso. "She clearly knows the world of intelligence. But the Russians are old hands at disinformation, so our meeting might not be as accidental as she claims. It could be a cover for some devious setup."

Spicer requested and paid the check.

"I'm off to see MI5," he said. "I won't mention your being here.

And I'll send the memo to Ted. Can you stay on in London a little longer?"

"I think so, sure."

The station chief stood up and flashed Malko a piratical grin. "You and I have worked a lot of jobs together, and it would be fun if this one panned out. But I can't see the Agency agreeing to a targeted assassination, even for a whole bunch of Russian spies. We don't do that sort of thing anymore."

Once out on the Grosvenor Square sidewalk, Malko thought of calling his old pal Gwyneth Robertson. A retired CIA case officer, Gwyneth was the queen of high-society fellatio, perfected in the best British finishing schools.

But then he had a better idea.

Why not call "the bitch," Lynn Marsh? If the swallows project took off, being in touch with her could be useful.

The call to Lynn's number went to voice mail, so Malko left a message inviting her to dinner. It felt like tossing a bottle with a note into the sea.

Thanks to Zhanna, he knew that the young dentist was currently on her own in London, since Alexei was in New York. Malko might be able to determine if she was as much in love with him as Zhanna feared.

Rem Tolkachev slowly reread the short memo. It had reached him after a circuit of several thousand miles in absolute secrecy. It was just one page, single spaced, but its author demanded immediate action.

Tolkachev made a habit of always reading important documents twice, to really absorb them. Sometimes he would discover a new angle on the repeat reading. Caution and care were second nature to him. They had allowed him to keep his small office in the south wing of the Kremlin for the last sixteen years.

His door bore no sign, and only its thickness and sophisticated access code—it changed every week and was known only to Tolkachev and one presidential aide—suggested that the office housed someone important. The few people in the Kremlin who knew called it Osobié Svyazi, the Office of Special Affairs.

Over the years, Tolkachev had served a succession of Kremlin masters: Gorbachev, Yeltsin, Putin, and now Medvedev. The latter didn't take much notice of the old man and let his prime minister, Vladimir Putin, deal with him.

Tolkachev served all those masters with the same dedication. In his eyes, he was working for his *rodina*, Russia. The only leader to officially recognize him was Yuri Andropov, the former KGB head, who awarded him the Order of Lenin.

It hadn't gone to his head. Tolkachev was a soldier of the shadows, devoted and dispassionate.

The steel-reinforced safe in his office contained the leadership's most explosive secrets of the last quarter century. Most of the instructions Tolkachev gave were oral. When a written document was required, he wrote it by hand or typed a single copy on an old Remington, an American Lend-Lease gift. The spymaster deeply distrusted electronic media, and saw the Internet as a trap invented by the imperialists. He hadn't ever wanted a secretary.

If, against all odds, someone managed to break into his office, a powerful incendiary device would burn up the intruder along with the room and all its precious documents.

Every morning Tolkachev drove into the Kremlin through the Borovitskiy gate. He used to drive an old Volga but had recently been given a brand-new Lada, whose modern lines he hated. In the evening he returned to a modest apartment on Kastanaev-skaya Street in a quiet Moscow neighborhood. A widower, he ate at home except when he indulged his only weakness, going to the Bolshoi.

Tolkachev carefully folded the document he'd just read and filed it in the large wall safe. He glanced at his large poster of Felix Dzerzhinsky, published in 1926 on the Cheka founder's death. The man he admired most in the world. The one who reportedly said, "There are no innocents in the socialist state, only bad investigators." Tolkachev often went to the KGB museum on Lubyanka Street to contemplate Dzerzhinsky's death mask.

Just then someone knocked on the door, and the red warning light came on. Tolkachev checked the peephole to identify his visitor, but it was only the fat housekeeper who brought him the sweetened tea he drank every day around four thirty. Her eyes downcast, she set the tray on his empty desk and silently beat a retreat.

Tolkachev sipped his tea and pondered his next course of action. He disliked haste and recklessness, whose results almost always had to be corrected later.

He picked up his telephone and dialed the number of one of President Medvedev's aides. This was Tolkachev's liaison with Vladimir Putin, who had been exiled to the white prime minister's building.

Tolkachev's phone was connected to the internal Kremlin network but wasn't listed in the official directory. The only people who could call him were those he'd given the number to. On the other hand, all the numbers *he* might need were contained in a locked address book. It held the names of two generations of apparatchiks and intelligence agents.

When a senior official in one of the major departments was

promoted, he was immediately told about Rem Stalievitch Tolkachev. Few knew what he looked like, or much beyond his somewhat slow speech and high-pitched voice, with an accent from central Russia. What they did know was that when Tolkachev asked for something, he was to get it immediately, without asking questions. He embodied the Kremlin's absolute power, regardless of who the current tsar might be.

Born the son of an NKVD general at Sverdlovsk in 1934, Tolkachev had spent his entire career in the "organs." This included a long stint in the KGB's Second Directorate, where he was the liaison with the elite military Alpha group. This gave him an endless supply of efficient, discreet, and reliable assassins.

Tolkachev didn't make much of an impression on people who didn't know his real functions. Widowed for a decade, he was a tiny old gentleman with a crown of smooth white hair. But he ruled not only departments and intelligence agencies. Over the years he had accumulated a prodigious collection of contacts that allowed him to confront any situation.

His safe held thousands of files, their pages dense with his tiny, precise writing about all the people he'd ever used. They were all there: *siloviki*, gangsters, killers, swindlers, mafiosi, bankers, military veterans, and priests, in intimate detail.

Tolkachev always knew exactly whom he was dealing with.

Every month, he combed through his list, drawing a little Orthodox cross by the names of people who had died.

He was the person who had had the idea of launching a new flight of *lastochkas* fourteen years earlier.

When the SVR succeeded the glorious First Directorate, all the best operatives left the agency to go into the private sector and get rich.

Dismayed by the foreign intelligence service's incompetence, Tolkachev sent a letter under seal to Vladimir Putin. To his surprise, he was summoned to the president's office that very day. The Kremlin's new leader was a man who shared both Tolkachev's hatred of Gorbachev and his nostalgia for the days of Soviet power.

"Rem Stalievitch, Russia should have many more men like you!" exclaimed Putin. "I approve your project 200 percent. What do you require?"

"Only your support, Mr. President. I'll do the rest."

Thanks to a complex, top-secret routing system, Tolkachev had unlimited funds at his disposal, in cash or any other payment method, everywhere in the world. It required no accounting, but Tolkachev was compulsively honest and wouldn't steal a kopeck from the money at his disposal. His greatest joy came from the unlimited power he exercised and the trust shown him by the country's leadership.

His only distraction was a monthly visit to the Bolshoi. He bought his own ticket, though a mere phone call would've opened up an entire row of orchestra seats. And his only indulgence was the slim, pastel-colored Sobranie Cocktail cigarettes he chain-smoked when he was thinking hard.

Having finished his sweet tea, Tolkachev lit one now.

He had to give his correspondent an answer by this evening, but he was in a quandary. The *lastochkas* network was his pet project. Over two years, he had personally recruited all its members, choosing them with the greatest care. Each had family back in Russia, which gave Tolkachev leverage over them, but none had misbehaved.

Good Russians still existed, he reflected.

Early on, his first problem arose when the man Tolkachev appointed as the link with the agents in the United States got cancer. Boris Orlov was a businessman who'd made a fortune plundering Russia's nickel industry, so he did whatever the authorities asked of him. Nor was Orlov suspect in American eyes. He had officially broken all ties with the motherland and lived in the United States, which was essential.

Alas, Orlov now lay buried with the others who had served the nation in Moscow's prestigious Novodevichy Cemetery.

Tolkachev had learned of Alexei Khrenkov while leafing through the secret reports delivered to him every morning. The spymaster investigated, and learned that he'd swindled his way to a fortune and was about to flee the country. Seeing that the former vice minister would have the perfect profile of a network leader, Tolkachev had made his move.

Khrenkov was about to board his flight at Sheremetyevo International Airport when he was taken aside by customs officials for a supposedly routine check. Instead, he spent that night in the Lubyanka prison basement. They left him there for a week with practically nothing to eat, giving Tolkachev time to study his reaction. Then they took him from his cell, cleaned him up, and brought him to the Kremlin.

In an anonymous office, Khrenkov had met a white-haired old man who gave him a stark choice: become the head of the swallows network or join Putin's defeated rival Mikhail Khodorkovsky in Siberia for the next fifteen years.

Unlike Khodorkovsky, Khrenkov actually was guilty.

Tolkachev warned him that he would be under constant surveillance by security agents. That wasn't unusual; all the émigré oligarchs had bodyguards. The difference was that these men would be taking their orders from the Kremlin.

Needless to say, Khrenkov had jumped at the chance. There wasn't even a handshake to seal the deal; these people were serious. He was told he was free to leave the country, and had best do it quickly, because the Moscow oblast was starting to realize what the Khrenkovs had done. So he flew out of Sheremetyevo without any problem, leaving Russia for good.

It was none too soon. Three days later, the oblast obtained a warrant for his arrest, as did the Moscow FSB financial section. Neither organization knew about the deal Khrenkov and Tolkachev had struck, of course. In their eyes, he was just another rich fugitive.

Just the same, the Kremlin passed word to the FSB not to broadcast the affair abroad, so as not to scare off foreign investors.

In the three years since, everything had worked perfectly. The swallows network was beginning to produce results. One of the spies, a gorgeous redhead, had even married a U.S. senator thirty years her senior who sat on a number of important committees.

If Tolkachev drank champagne, he would have raised a glass.

Today, however, he found himself facing a completely unexpected problem.

If it had involved anyone other than Malko Linge, he wouldn't have worried. But he particularly distrusted the CIA agent, who had given him a lot of grief in the past. Linge's meeting Khrenkov and his wife couldn't possibly be a coincidence. As a follower of scientific socialism, Tolkachev didn't believe in coincidences.

It would be easy enough to have the agent killed, but something held Tolkachev back. Though he doubted it, the meeting actually could have been a coincidence. And in that case, killing Linge would draw attention to the Khrenkovs, which was the last thing he wanted.

By his sixth cigarette, he'd made up his mind. His reasoning was logical. If the CIA agent had actually met the lord of the swallows by chance, he would soon move on, and everything would return to normal.

If not, it would prove that the CIA was after something. That would be extremely unfortunate, because it would mean Khrenkov had been targeted. It might be for the "wrong" reasons, such as his recent and very shady past. But it might also be for his role running the network.

In which case Tolkachev would have to act very quickly.

He would first kill Linge, then bring Khrenkov home. It would leave the network leaderless, but that was better than scuttling it. Tolkachev had no illusions about people. If the Americans gave Khrenkov a choice between betraying his network or spending the next hundred and fifty years in prison, he wouldn't hesitate for a second. He was no hero of the Soviet Union, just a crooked apparatchik who wanted to enjoy his ill-gotten gains.

Tolkachev stubbed out his last cigarette unfinished and drafted a short note to the head of the Khrenkovs' protection detail. This was Vladimir Krazovsky, a former Spetsnaz colonel and devoted patriot whose job was to maintain a firewall around the couple to make sure they made no further suspicious contacts.

Malko had long since returned to the Lanesborough, and he was feeling at loose ends. Gwyneth Robertson, his friend with benefits in London, was on assignment in Stockholm for her think tank and wouldn't be back for another three days. And Lynn Marsh still hadn't answered his message.

He decided to call her again, though without much hope. To Malko's surprise, she answered on the fifth ring.

"Hello."

"Hi, there. It's Malko Linge," he said in his most seductive voice. "I left you a message earlier."

It took the young dentist a few seconds to place him.

"Oh, of course! You were the man at my table last night."

"That's right. I suggested we have a drink at Annabel's, but you said no."

"I had to get up early this morning."

"The message I left was to invite you to dinner tonight."

"I haven't checked my mobile. Sorry."

"So what do you say?"

She agreed, but with some reluctance.

"I've had a tiring day, and will have to get home early. Could we have dinner at seven?"

"Absolutely. How shall we meet? Can I pick you up?"

"No, I have my car. Where are you staying?"

"At the Lanesborough."

"All right, I'll see you there at seven. You can choose the restaurant."

Malko hung up, feeling half-satisfied. Lynn didn't have anything untoward in mind. Zhanna was right: she really was in love with Alexei Khrenkov.

CHAPTER
8

Lynn Marsh nibbled the last of her rhubarb crumble and ginger ice cream and looked at Malko with an expression of delight.

"This is marvelous!"

Annabel's was as pleasant as ever. Their table stood a little distance from the small dance floor and the booths occupied by people who were there only for cocktails. The music was neither too loud nor too modern, and when the band started playing "Strangers in the Night," Malko took the opportunity to ask Lynn to dance.

After the slightest of hesitations, she stood up and preceded Malko down the few stairs to the dance floor. This gave him a perfect view of her back. She was wearing a long white dress that emphasized her tan, open to the top of her buttocks.

When Malko put his arm around her, setting his hand low on her bare back, she pulled away slightly.

Aside from his somewhat formally kissing her hand, this was the first time they'd actually touched.

They danced very properly, with Lynn holding herself erect and a little apart. She was the first to head back to their table, where a bottle of Taittinger Brut in a silver bucket awaited them.

"I love champagne!" she said.

Like most women.

The champagne seemed to loosen her up more than dinner had, and Malko decided to see what he could learn.

"Are you seeing anybody these days?" he asked casually.

"Yes."

"He gives you a lot of freedom," he said, with a touch of irony.

Lynn took his remark literally.

"He doesn't live in London. He's traveling right now."

"Was he supposed to have been in my seat at the gala last night?"

"That's right."

This confirmed what Zhanna Khrenkov had told him. Lynn was indeed her husband's mistress. Malko didn't pursue the matter; he knew enough. In any case, the young dentist glanced at her watch as she drank a final flute of champagne.

"I can't stay out too late," she said. "Do you mind if we leave now?"

Malko assured her he didn't mind and asked for the check. Waiting for a taxi under Annabel's awning, he looked the young woman over, thinking that it was too bad she was involved with someone else.

"I'll get off with you at the Lanesborough," she said. "I left my car with the valet parking there. I live quite far away, beyond Hammersmith."

Vladimir Krazovsky was parked at the corner of Charles Street, at the wheel of a gray Golf belonging to his nominal employer, Petropavlovsk.

He was watching the entrance of Annabel's and saw Lynn Marsh when she emerged. He'd been tailing her since she left her home. The orders had come from Moscow that morning: stick close to Dr. Marsh and make note of everyone she saw.

Krazovsky hadn't been able to drive into Harrods Village, where she lived. It was a gated community with a guard, so he'd been forced to wait outside. When Lynn drove by in her gray Mercedes convertible, he waited a moment before following it down Trinity Church Road and then Castlenau, which was empty.

It was only after crossing the old Hammersmith Bridge that he encountered a little traffic. He watched as his "customer" entrusted her Mercedes to a bowler-hatted Lanesborough valet parker. He then quickly turned onto Grosvenor Crescent so he could circle around and park near the hotel entrance.

Krazovsky was surprised when Marsh promptly came back out, now accompanied by someone he had no trouble identifying: the man he had beaten in the Hôtel de Paris elevator on Alexei Khrenkov's orders.

He followed their taxi to Annabel's, and had been waiting nearby since. From time to time he drove around Berkeley Square, because police patrols were vigilant in these days of high terrorist alert. A car and driver that remained parked in the same place for too long looked suspicious and was likely to be checked.

He knew the couple was now heading to the Lanesborough, so Krazovsky let their taxi get some distance ahead of him. There, he watched as the young woman bid her date good night and retrieved her car. A less conscientious man wouldn't have bothered following her on the highway back to Hammersmith, but Krazovsky had been properly trained.

Malko gazed thoughtfully as the taillights of Lynn's Mercedes merged with the Brompton Road traffic. All in all, his evening had been well spent, even if it wasn't personally rewarding. The young woman's thoughts were elsewhere, and she hadn't responded to his discreet flirtation.

There weren't many dentists in London who could afford a Mercedes convertible. It represented thousands of mouths worked on. The existence of the luxury car was certainly a clue. It was a typical gift from a millionaire in love.

Once again, umbrellas were blooming in London. The weather had been terrible for the last two days. In a word, London-like.

Malko was feeling restless, especially since Alexandra was now growing unduly suspicious of his extended stay. Malko assured her that he was only waiting for the CIA's green light to leave, which happened to be absolutely true.

Stepping out of the shower, he wondered what he was going to do with his day.

The ringing of his cell pulled him from his morose mood.

"Did I wake you?" It was Richard Spicer's friendly voice.

"Almost."

"Tough luck. I'm sending you a car around noon. We're having lunch at the embassy."

The torment will finally be over, Malko thought. He would be able to return to his castle and to Alexandra, whom he promptly called.

She was out in the vineyards, and the connection was poor.

"Are you coming back today?" she asked.

"I think so."

"That's good timing! The Von Thyssens have invited us to dinner."

Gunther von Thyssen was another of Alexandra's many admirers. As if she could read Malko's thoughts, she proceeded smoothly:

"If you can't make it back, I'll go alone. I don't want to disappoint Gunther."

Bitch! Malko said to himself. Alexandra had a gift for perfectly maintaining the tension between them. She was well aware that knowing other men desired her turned Malko on.

"I'll be there!" he assured her. "I'd like you to wear your Dior suit, the one with the skirt slit up the side." "Your wish is my command!" she said sarcastically. "I'll wear the suit, but you better get here, because a lot of men seem to like it."

On that veiled threat, they hung up.

Having traveled by a secure and complicated route, an email had just reached Rem Tolkachev: an hour-by-hour account of the surveillance on Lynn Marsh.

What it told him was deeply troubling. Alexei Khrenkov's mistress had seen the CIA agent again! True, it was only for a dinner, but why had she wanted to see him for a second time? There was still a small chance that it was just a social or a romantic impulse. After all, Marsh was a very attractive woman.

But the idea that a CIA agent should be getting close to his *lastochkas* nest made Tolkachev extremely nervous. He had to warn Khrenkov. Marsh knew nothing of Alexei's role in the spy ring, so she may have sinned out of ignorance.

Still, Tolkachev had to be careful not to bring everything crashing down by acting hastily. The CIA would be keeping a close watch on a mission leader like Linge. If something happened to him, they would want to know why.

In his tiny handwriting, Tolkachev wrote a brief note to the Petropavlovsk branch in New York, where Khrenkov was.

The company, which exported crab and smoked fish, was an invaluable cover. Now run by the Kremlin, it was an old KGB shell company that had never been identified. Because it had branches in several major capitals, it was an unrivaled communication network.

Richard Spicer had dropped Malko off at the American embassy, which was as well guarded as Fort Knox. It was patrolled by officers of Scotland Yard's Special Branch, with weapons at the ready and radio links to an emergency center. In their dark body armor, the men looked like turtles.

Ushered into the CIA station chief's office, Malko found an unknown man already there, sitting in an armchair and reading the *Times*. He was about fifty, wore glasses, and had a big leather briefcase at his feet. An anonymous bureaucrat type.

The man stood up when Malko came in, and Spicer introduced them.

"This is Irving Boyd. He flew in this morning from Washington. He didn't get much sleep on the 777, so try not to rattle him."

"I wouldn't dream of it," said Malko, shaking Boyd's hand.

"Irving runs the Russia branch at the Directorate of Intelligence," Spicer continued. "He came to London especially to meet you."

"We're very interested in what you've learned," said Boyd, giving Malko a smile.

Malko, who realized he wouldn't be accompanying Alexandra to the Von Thyssens' that evening, said nothing.

A CIA counterintelligence chief flying across the Atlantic to meet him meant the Agency took Zhanna Khrenkov's proposal very seriously.

CHAPTER

9

Engrossed by Malko's account, the two Americans in the embassy dining room hadn't touched their smoked salmon appetizer. The Marine waiter served them an excellent Pouilly Fumé, then left.

Malko sipped his wine after describing Zhanna Khrenkov's offer in detail.

"As soon as I got Richard's message I opened our file on the Khrenkovs," said Irving Boyd. "The FBI provided the most useful material. They didn't have much on Alexei, but a lot on Zhanna.

"She arrived in New York on an Aeroflot flight on March 13, 1991. She first lived in Coney Island with a Ukrainian woman. Worked as a live-in nanny for a few families, and eventually for a couple named Bartok, who had two children, on the Upper East Side. After she had been with them a year, John Bartok divorced his wife. He married Zhanna six months later." Boyd paused. "To judge by the photos, she was a very good-looking blonde."

"A pretty typical story," said Malko.

"The FBI investigated her, of course, but didn't turn up anything," continued Boyd. "Then there's a gap in her bio. Next she appears in Moscow in 1993, traveling on an American passport in the name of Bartok, though she'd gotten divorced six months earlier. She had enough alimony to live on for five years."

"Do we know why she got divorced?" asked Malko.

"Not really. We checked the Brooklyn court records, and they mention irreconcilable differences. It went through pretty fast; not much to get excited about."

Falling silent, the three men turned their attention to the smoked salmon. When their plates were empty, Boyd continued his account.

"Zhanna renewed her American passport in 1995 at our Moscow consulate. That's about the time she met Alexei Khrenkov, who was working at Inkombank.

"For the 1995 to 2000 period, the Moscow station only has the Russian files, and they're pretty slim. I suspect the Khrenkovs were being left alone. Zhanna wasn't working. Probably living on the money Alexei was skimming from Inkombank.

"She traveled regularly to New York. With her American passport, that was no problem. She bought a brownstone on East Eighty-Third Street. She also got involved in cultural affairs, sponsoring an exhibit of Russian art at the Guggenheim Museum, which got her noticed, of course."

"Who paid for that?" asked Malko as the waiter cleared the table.

"Zhanna. She also brought a Russian philharmonic orchestra to the city. Meanwhile she continued to travel between Moscow and New York."

The waiter brought the men slabs of roast beef so succulent you could grab and tear them to pieces with your bare hands.

"What about Alexei during this time?" asked Malko.

Boyd waited for the waiter to leave before answering.

"We don't know a whole lot about him. Before you brought him to our attention he didn't appear in any Agency files."

"Anybody else's?"

"The FBI told us what they had: practically nothing," said

Boyd. "Two years ago he and Zhanna paid eleven million dollars for the place on Eighty-Third Street. The money came from a Cayman Islands account. The FBI saw Khrenkov as a minor oligarch, a Russian businessman who'd gotten rich. And of course nobody's gotten rich honestly there for the last twenty years.

"When Khrenkov left Russia for good in 2008, we didn't know anything about him. The Moscow station alerted us to his financial exploits."

"How much did he steal?"

"The Russians put it in the billions, but we think it's less than that: about seven hundred million dollars. At least that's what some banker friends in Moscow say."

"But if Khrenkov was considered a crook, how was he able to enter the United States?" asked Malko.

"Good question," said Boyd, pausing to finish the last of his roast beef. "The Russian authorities didn't issue an international arrest warrant against him, for some reason. So he isn't wanted by Interpol, and outside of Russia he's presumed innocent. The Russians have never asked us any questions about him.

"Besides, as the husband of an American citizen, we couldn't bar him entry to the United States. The FBI knows about his activities from their Moscow office, of course. They sent his file to Immigration with a strong recommendation not to issue him an American passport. For now, he's using his Russian one. It's still valid, and Moscow hasn't canceled it."

A hush fell on the group. The story had so many strange twists and turns, they realized the Khrenkovs should have come to official notice a long time ago.

"So the Agency never took an interest in Alexei before you got my message?" asked Malko.

"Never," said Boyd.

"He would be an ideal candidate to run a spy network," said

Malko. "The fact that he can't go back to Russia on pain of arrest puts him above suspicion."

"Of course."

"I guess if Mikhail Khodorkovsky got out of Siberia and moved to the United States, no one would suspect him, either. His status as a fugitive would give him the perfect cover."

"That assumes that some of Zhanna Khrenkov's story is true," Boyd pointed out a bit nervously.

"Look, Irving, if you doubted her story, you wouldn't have crossed the Atlantic to come see me," said Malko.

The hush descended again. People in counterintelligence were always so strange, both paranoid and naïve. Even though the Aldrich Ames case showed that the truth can be right under their noses.

Boyd was silent for a few moments, then looked over at Malko.

"Counterintelligence is my beat," he said, "so I can't dismiss the possibility of a spy ring operating in our country, even if I don't believe it."

Richard Spicer, who had been silent until then, spoke up.

"What do you make of it, Malko?"

He thought for a moment, then said:

"I know the Russians well enough to be cautious. Zhanna could certainly have cooked up this story to put something over on us. She sure hates Lynn Marsh, so that part of the story is credible."

He described the evening he'd spent with Marsh the night before, then said:

"Zhanna seems to know a lot about the intelligence services, but that doesn't mean anything. Right now, I couldn't say whether a network exists or if she's putting me on."

A very long silence followed.

Malko turned to Boyd, and asked:

"Does the existence of a clandestine spy ring strike you as plausible?"

"It's not impossible," said Boyd cautiously. "The Russians used plenty of sleeper agents in the old days. They called them *lastochkas*, 'swallows.' We identified some of them, but not all."

"But with the improvement in our relations, the network theory seems less likely. President Obama would be furious if he discovered that such a spy ring existed, and it would have serious consequences."

"Like what?" countered Malko. "Benjamin Netanyahu made him lose face over the settlements issue, and he didn't do anything about it."

Boyd looked down in embarrassment.

"So what do we do now?" asked Spicer after the waiter brought the men coffee.

"We have to determine if the network really exists," said Boyd, reviving a bit.

Malko couldn't help smiling.

"Of course, but how?"

The silence returned, thick as molasses. Then the counterintelligence chief spoke.

"We have to pretend to be interested in Zhanna Khrenkov's proposal but make her prove she has something to peddle."

"What kind of proof do you want?"

"I have no idea," he admitted. "You know this affair better than I do."

Malko rolled his eyes. Even if Zhanna gave him proof that the mysterious network existed, they still faced a major obstacle. Was the CIA really prepared to kill an innocent young woman to shut it down?

Malko doubted it.

In any case, the next step was up to him.

Boyd glanced at his watch.

"I have an appointment with MI5 at three. That's the official reason for my trip. I'm heading back to Washington tonight. Richard will pass on whatever you find out. And if need be, I can send you my deputy. He knows Russia well and speaks the language."

"Are you going to mention this business to MI5?" asked Malko. Boyd nearly choked.

"Of course not. Not to anybody, not even our Moscow station. If the network exists, we'll want to come down on it like a Predator drone. This calls for absolute secrecy. Aside from the three of us, nobody knows."

Standing up, Boyd gave Malko a warm handshake but an apologetic smile.

"The Russians are pros, Malko. I can't see them running a network with people who would betray them over something as trivial as a marital problem."

Malko couldn't help but smile.

"You don't know what a jealous woman is like, Irving. She'll destroy the world to get rid of her rival. On that point, I don't doubt how much Zhanna hates Alexei's girlfriend."

The counterintelligence chief didn't answer.

Entering the Dorchester, Malko passed a fat Arab woman in hijab who was struggling to squeeze through the revolving door with a half dozen enormous bags from Louis Vuitton, Dolce & Gabbana, Hermès, and Valentino. Without the doorman's help, she would never have managed.

Another fashion victim, Malko thought sadly.

Once in the lobby, which housed a tea shop and a bar, Malko turned right and walked to the elevators. He was going downstairs.

He came out on a hall with blue wallpaper and a sign that read "The Spa at the Dorchester" in silver letters.

A little farther, a staircase to the left led down to the spa proper, while a door opened to the fitness area. The stairs brought Malko to a small room with beige fabric on the walls and a big sofa. The hostess was a charming Asian woman, as slender as a reed.

"What can I do for you, sir?" she asked, a little surprised to see a man there.

Malko gave her a reassuring smile.

"I'd like to leave a message for one of your clients who is coming by today, Mrs. Zhanna Khrenkov."

The young woman opened a register and glanced at it.

"Yes, she has an appointment at six o'clock."

Malko took the envelope he'd prepared from his pocket.

"See that she gets this, please."

After window shopping for a while, Malko walked back to the Lanesborough. He would have to call Alexandra and give her the bad news that he was extending his stay in London.

"Those spooks are always screwing up your life," Alexandra said with a sigh. "Too bad. I was just thinking about wearing that suit you like. It goes beautifully with gray stockings. I'll be thinking about you."

In Malko's mind, the warning lights were all flashing red. Alexandra wasn't using the caustic tone she usually took when blaming him for something. That was worrisome. His absence clearly wasn't breaking her heart.

"Behave yourself," he said without conviction. "I'll be home very soon."

"Have fun with your spooks!" she said coolly, and hung up.

Malko only waited thirty seconds before calling Gwyneth

Robertson. He got her voice mail again but figured she would have to show up sooner or later. He could always try his luck with Lynn Marsh, but she really didn't seem receptive.

Just then his cell rang. He prayed that it would be Gwyneth and the promise of a pleasant evening. Unfortunately, it was Zhanna Khrenkov's somewhat harsh voice.

Without preamble, she said:

"I'll meet you for dinner at the Dorchester's Chinese restaurant. It's in the back on the left, opposite the bar."

CHAPTER

10

Compared to Lynn Marsh, Zhanna Khrenkov was a frump.
She had her hair in a bun and no makeup on. In ballet flats, she
looked even shorter than usual. When Malko thought of Lynn's
sophisticated beauty, he could understand Alexei's infidelity.

Zhanna had chosen their meeting site well. The China Tang
was at the end of the hall downstairs, and not easy to find. The
dining room, with its tasteful Asian décor, was empty.

She had arrived before him, and was seated in a dark alcove
where they wouldn't be seen.

When they'd ordered, Zhanna shot him an amused look.

"Your friends are taking me seriously, aren't they?"

"What makes you say that?"

"Otherwise you wouldn't be here. Have they accepted my
offer?"

Malko had to admit she certainly had nerve.

"We're not there yet," answered Malko carefully. "I passed on
your proposal, that's all."

"So?"

"The Agency isn't convinced your network actually exists."

Zhanna waited until the waitress set out their bowls of soup,
then remarked caustically:

"But they sort of believe it."

"These aren't people who act on hunches, Zhanna. They need proof that the network exists. And if you don't provide it, our involvement ends now."

Malko sampled his crab and asparagus soup. The restaurant's setting was none too cheerful, but the food was delicious.

Zhanna savored her hot and sour soup without looking at him. Then she put down her porcelain spoon and asked:

"What do they need as proof?"

"A few names."

Her look was cold, almost hostile.

"Malko, please. You keep treating me like a ninny. People don't show their cards ahead of time in this business. You just have to believe me. I'll say only this: a dozen swallows are now operating in the United States. And two of them have made judicious marriages that put them in a position to learn information of great interest to the Russian government."

"Get serious, Zhanna! Do you expect the Agency to start examining every questionable marriage between a Russian and an influential American?"

Malko dug into his lemon chicken and Zhanna her spring rolls. Neither spoke until they had finished their entrees and drunk the last of the tea.

Malko called for the check. He was annoyed at having stood Alexandra up for nothing. It was only when he was putting his American Express card away that Zhanna spoke again.

"Does the name Rem Tolkachev mean anything to you?"

He looked up in surprise.

"No, why?"

Zhanna looked at him almost scornfully.

"He's the man who created the network," she whispered. "On Vladimir Putin's direct order, to make up for the SVR's incompetence."

She seemed irritated, and Malko sensed she wasn't trying to mislead him.

"All right, tell me more. What agency is he with?"

Zhanna shook her head.

"That's all I'm going to say. Give your friends that name, and if they're interested, come see me again."

With that, she grabbed her purse and strode briskly out the door. Malko didn't try to catch up with her. When he left in turn, the waitress gave him a sympathetic smile, sure she had just witnessed a lovers' quarrel.

Alexei Khrenkov's face lit up when he saw Lynn Marsh standing in the restaurant door. The Park Terrace was on the top floor of the Royal Garden Hotel on Kensington High Street. A very British place where Khrenkov wasn't likely to run into anyone he knew.

Smiling brightly, Lynn walked toward his table. She was wearing a Chanel-style black-and-white wool jacket, a tight black skirt and stockings, and a pair of Jimmy Choo shoes that Khrenkov had bought for her.

She stepped into his arms, and they hugged for a few moments under the other diners' discreet stares. Such public displays of affection were rare in such a conservative place.

Khrenkov led her to the table and sat her down without releasing her hand.

"God, you're beautiful!" he murmured, unable to take his eyes off her.

"I missed you," she said simply.

When the waiter came for their order, they both opted for filet of sole, the safest choice among the menu's dangerously "British" entrees.

"When did you get in?" she asked.

"This morning. I stopped by the apartment to drop off my things, then I went to the office."

"Did you see her?"

"No. She was sleeping."

Khrenkov gazed at her, mesmerized. Lynn was so beautiful, he thought, her eyes so full of life.

"I want you very badly," he whispered.

"I've arranged things with my office mate," she said with a secret smile. "My first patient isn't until five o'clock."

"That's wonderful. I reserved us a suite here."

Lynn gave him a playful smile.

"We could have eaten lunch upstairs."

Richard Spicer reread the short message he was about to send to Langley. It mentioned Rem Tolkachev, the name Zhanna had provided as proof of her claim. It hadn't rung a bell with Spicer, either.

"I'm sending the information encrypted to Irving," said the CIA station chief. "For the time being there's nothing to do but wait. When will you see Mrs. Khrenkov again?"

"I'm to leave her a message at the Dorchester Spa."

Spicer gave him a searching look.

"What do you think of her story?" he asked.

"There's something to it, but it'll be tough to cut a deal. Zhanna obviously won't hand over the network for nothing, assuming there is one. Let's see what Langley has to say."

"Care to have dinner tonight?" asked Spicer.

"Thanks, but I already have an engagement."

Malko didn't say that it was with Gwyneth Robertson, the former case officer. Having left the CIA, Gwyneth was now a highly paid partner in a think tank. She was also a world-class slut. For

Gwyneth, having sex was as natural as brushing her teeth, and she did it with a class you couldn't help but admire.

Khrenkov slipped the magnetic card into the lock. When the green light blinked, he opened the door, revealing a large living room.

"It's huge!" Lynn exclaimed.

She didn't get much time to admire the spacious suite, however. Khrenkov already had hold of her, shoving his hips against her and grabbing at her breasts.

"Jesus, you're an animal!" she cried with a smile. Specifically, a ram in heat.

Pressed against her, Khrenkov could feel a monstrous erection rapidly rising. Unable to ignore it, Lynn turned around and started passionately kissing him.

Panting, Khrenkov fumbled under her skirt, reached to the top of a stocking to find naked flesh. She wasn't wearing pantyhose, for which he mentally thanked her.

Yanking his zipper down so hard it nearly ripped, Khrenkov liberated a cock that was already pointed at the ceiling. Lynn promptly grabbed and started stroking him, but he stopped her.

"No, don't!" he grunted. "You'll make me come!"

He dragged her into the bedroom. Lynn sat down gracefully on the bed but was given no time to undress. Before she could even take off her Chanel jacket, Khrenkov was already tipping her backward.

Having shoved up Lynn's skirt, he pulled her black nylon panties down her legs—they wound up dangling from an ankle—and fell onto her with a groan of delight, roughly parting her legs with his knee.

Half laughing, half shocked, Lynn yielded to the sexual tornado.

"Go easy, darling!" she begged.

Khrenkov was already inside her, and she gave a little cry when she felt him plumbing her depths, trying to go even deeper.

Now he was on his knees, pants halfway down his legs, and thudding at her like a woodcutter. Like her, he was still wearing his jacket. As if to spread her even wider, he pinned her legs under his muscular thighs and pressed them into the bedclothes.

His mouth crushing hers, their teeth bumping, he pounded away. Lynn was barely aware of his two-hundred-odd pounds of muscle. Though Khrenkov didn't seem to notice, her cunt had begun to stream like a fountain. The rough sex had triggered an irresistible orgasm that went on and on under the battering. She wrapped her arms tightly around his back, holding him tight, and screamed with pleasure.

Turning her head, she caught a glimpse of them reflected in the wardrobe mirror. Her skirt was up around her waist, revealing a strip of pale skin above her stockings. The sight excited her even more. If she could move, she would have raised her hips to take her lover in even deeper, but he'd flattened her like a pancake.

Suddenly Khrenkov froze, as if struck by lightning. Lynn felt the rush of his orgasm fill her and she cried out again. He slumped down, his mouth against her neck. After a long moment, he pulled away, muttering a few words in Russian, and rolled onto his back, his cock still proudly erect.

Completely shameless.

In a daze, Lynn closed her thighs, got rid of her black skirt, and stumbled to the bathroom.

Before meeting Alexei, she had never made love with such violence and intensity. As she stripped off her stained clothes, she couldn't help wondering whether he had ever made love this way to his wife, in the old days.

———

Zhanna Khrenkov stood at the window smoking a cigarette and gazing across Grosvenor Place to the leafy Buckingham Palace grounds. Tourists were making their way along the razor-wire-topped fence to admire the lake and the back of the palace. If they were looking for the famous, much-photographed changing of the guard, they were out of luck, because it was around on the other side.

Zhanna was feeling dissatisfied with her meeting with Malko. There wasn't much more she could do in negotiating with the CIA, but thinking about it now, her idea seemed completely crazy.

She knew she was taking—and making Alexei take—a huge risk. Even if by some miracle her ploy succeeded, they would have the Kremlin on their heels, with all the menace that entailed.

Vladimir Putin would never forgive them. If there was one kind of person he hated, it was a traitor. He never made peace with them. His former ally Boris Berezovsky had left Russia a decade earlier, but the master of the Kremlin still dreamed of killing him.

Zhanna stubbed her cigarette out in an Hermès ashtray and walked into Alexei's bedroom. His luggage had barely been opened. Irina, the Moldovan maid, gave her a polite smile as she unpacked the bags.

Zhanna had only pretended to be asleep when he'd arrived from New York, so as not to force him to lie. She knew Alexei would be with that bitch, and was probably making love to her right now.

With the same energy he once brought to having sex with her, light-years ago.

His extraordinary sexual power was what had first attracted her to him. Zhanna wasn't a particularly sensual woman, but Alexei could have awakened a corpse. And she was sure he retained that same sexual energy now, twenty years later, when he hardly ever touched her anymore. Just imagining him sprawled on top of her rival, plowing her with his huge cock, gave her a sharp pain in the belly.

It felt like appendicitis.

But it was only hatred.

She suddenly started to pray that the CIA would accept her offer, in spite of the risks it entailed. She was cheered by the image of Lynn Marsh lying cold and dead in the metal drawer of some morgue. With Zhanna's steely will, she would succeed. Because she wasn't blowing smoke. If she could tell the Americans the truth about the *lastochkas* network, she would have them eating out of her hand.

Lynn emerged from the bathroom looking pink and fresh. She had taken a shower and dabbed on some perfume, then knotted a bath towel over her chest.

Khrenkov was still sprawled on the bed. He had taken off his coat and tie and unbuttoned his shirt. But he hadn't zipped up his pants, and his thick cock lay curved on his thigh. Seeing Lynn, he gave her a radiant smile and stretched out his arms.

"*Dushka!* Come here, quick. I miss you already."

Lynn approached the bed. The moment she was within reach, Alexei tore off the towel, then pulled her in tight and covered her with kisses.

She pretended to struggle, which increased his excitement. Moving her aside, he displayed his stiffening cock.

"Give me some help!" he whispered, taking Lynn's neck and pushing her head down.

"Wait! I'm going to draw the curtains!" she said, trying to free herself.

But her British modesty wasn't to Khrenkov's taste. With an iron grip, he forced Lynn's face down to his crotch. His cock quickly swelled, becoming too big for her mouth. Anyway, he'd never been a big fan of blow jobs, feeling that a man in love didn't need one to get a hard-on.

He stood up and pulled his shirt off—popping several buttons in the process—to reveal a muscular, hairy chest. Then he wriggled out of his pants and shoes.

Standing near the bed, Khrenkov gazed down at his mistress. While he was getting undressed, his erection had drooped a bit. Now he came close, holding his cock in his left hand, and presented it to her. This time he didn't have to use force; she wanted him again.

"Turn around," he ordered after a few moments.

Lynn obeyed, her face and chest down and her rump raised. When Khrenkov approached, he realized he was at just the right height. Without the slightest effort his cock parted Lynn's folds and, with a little push, entered her. He closed his large hands around her hips and shoved, sinking all the way in.

Feeling skewered, Lynn gave a shout. Alexei was already moving in and out, using all his strength. He gradually forced her down to the bed, where she lay prone. With a growl of irritation he grabbed a pillow and slipped it under her belly. When he penetrated her again, it was as forcefully as before. Leaning on his forearms, he plunged in and out almost vertically, as if doing push-ups.

Lynn moaned, torn between pain and incredible excitement. She had never experienced anything like it.

"Please come!" she begged him, feeling as if her pussy were being punished.

"I love how tight you hold me," muttered Alexei.

In a moment, he came inside her for the second time.

Later, he got up to light a cigarette. Lynn hated cigarette smoke, but she said nothing, trying not to breathe.

Now sated, Khrenkov turned and put his hand on her bare breast, as if taking possession of it.

"Was the evening at Christie's fun?" he asked.

"I wish you'd been there."

"So do I. Did you behave yourself?"

"How can you ask me that?" she snapped. "I called you a half hour later."

Alexei gave her a teasing smile.

"Yes, but on your cell phone. You might've been anywhere."

Seeing Lynn's outraged expression, Alexei leaned close and kissed her nipple.

"I'm joking!" he said. "I know you're faithful. Were your table-mates pleasant company, at least?"

"A Kazakh millionaire and an Austrian prince. He invited me to Annabel's afterward, but of course I said no."

"Did you see him again after that?"

Lynn opened her mouth to say yes, but closed it.

That was something you couldn't admit to a man as distrustful as Alexei Khrenkov, even though she hadn't done anything wrong.

"No, of course not."

Under Alexei's fingers, his mistress's skin suddenly felt cold. He remained perfectly calm, but he wanted to scream.

Thanks to the surveillance team, he knew she was lying.

She was hiding the fact that she had seen Malko Linge again, one of the CIA's most dangerous agents. It couldn't be a coincidence, and it had the most serious possible implications.

Alexei would have to protect the swallows at any price.

Torn between fury and anguish, he turned to look at Lynn Marsh's perfect profile. He knew he should probably strangle her on the spot but couldn't bring himself to do it.

He would have to try something different.

CHAPTER

11

Malko woke up in a bad mood. First, because the weather was lousy. What the British sarcastically call "liquid sunshine" was coming down in sheets. Second, because Gwyneth Robertson had stood him up the night before, though not deliberately. A wildcat strike at Air France grounded her flight, and she couldn't make it to London to have dinner with him. Malko was reduced to eating alone in the Lanesborough dining room.

He was getting sick and tired of London. The more he thought about it, the more far-fetched Zhanna Khrenkov's offer seemed. You don't trade a whole spy ring for a dead rival. Besides, there were plenty of killers for hire available in Russia. Unless something much more devious was going on.

To kill time, Malko went window shopping, wandering past the many luxury boutiques on Old Bond Street. He wound up having lunch in the Grill Room at the Connaught.

Over coffee, he phoned Richard Spicer.

The CIA station chief had news.

"We have a conference call scheduled for three this afternoon," he said. "I was about to ring you."

"Who's it with?" asked Malko.

"The person you met here the other day. That's all I can say now."

Malko still had half an hour to spare, so he decided to walk to Grosvenor Square. His mood hadn't improved by the time he reached the American embassy. But Spicer, possibly from the effects of a liquid lunch, seemed quite cheerful.

"Come with me to the yellow submarine," he said. "By the way, your friend Sir George Cornwell learned you're in London and is surprised not to have heard from you."

"I wanted to keep a low profile. What can I tell him?"

"The truth: that you're here on a matter that doesn't concern the cousins."

"That won't satisfy him. I don't want MI5's Section A3 people on me. You know, taking my picture and breaking into my hotel room."

"You're right," said Spicer. "Cornwell's a friend. Tell him part of the story. That we're trying to uncover a Russian network operating in the United States."

They were sitting in the embassy's small cipher room, which was equipped with several encrypted telephones. Spicer alerted the switchboard of their presence and at exactly three o'clock—ten a.m. in Washington, D.C.—a blinking red light on line three signaled an incoming call.

Spicer picked up and, after a few seconds, handed the phone to Malko.

"Irving wants to talk to you," he said. "I'll leave you to it."

"Good morning," said Malko. "Was the name I gave you of any interest?"

"Are you kidding? It rocked Langley to its foundations. Do you have any idea who Rem Tolkachev is?"

"No."

"He's the most senior and the most secretive member of the entire Russian espionage establishment. No photograph of him exists. Yet according to the very few defectors who have mentioned him, he's been on the job for more than fifteen years."

"What agency is he with?"

"That's just it: none of them. Tolkachev is his own agency, though he has contacts with the KGB, the GRU, and now the FSB."

"So who is his boss?" asked Malko.

"Vladimir Putin himself. Tolkachev has an office in the Kremlin, and he handles only special matters on the president's behalf. In other words, he's Putin's go-to guy for anything tricky and very secret. From decoded messages, we think he called the shots in the Litvinenko poisoning. In short, he's an extremely important person."

"Given that, does the fact that Zhanna Khrenkov gave us his name strike you as significant?"

"More than significant," said Boyd.

"Why? After all, she and her husband lived in Moscow until 2008. They could have heard about Tolkachev."

"That's not very likely. The only defectors to ever mention him in debriefings were very high ranking, at least general officers. The others didn't even know his name."

"So you think Zhanna Khrenkov's story might be true?"

"Yes, I do."

"So what do we do now?"

"Meet with Mrs. Khrenkov again and get her to put her cards on the table," said Boyd.

Malko found himself hovering between skepticism and despair.

"Irving, if she really works for Tolkachev, what makes you think she would sell him out?"

"She's not the one who works for him; it's her husband," said Boyd. "I talked with some of our profilers yesterday. The psychologists think that unconsciously, jealousy is driving her to take revenge on her husband."

"Does that mean I can say the Agency will kill her husband's girlfriend in exchange for giving us the network?"

"I'm afraid it's not that simple," said Boyd with a sigh. "You know very well that killing the Marsh woman is out of the question. When you see Mrs. Khrenkov, convince her that we take her seriously and try to work something out."

"I honestly don't see what good that would do," said Malko. "Zhanna's a tough cookie. We can't sell her a bill of goods."

"I'll leave it up to you. But I want to emphasize that we take this very seriously. President Obama has already been briefed on it."

"Listen, Irving, the SVR is already spying on the United States. Isn't that's enough? It's a big agency."

"Yeah, but we don't think their agents are very good," said Boyd. "Mikhail Fradkov is the head of the SVR. He's a former prime minister, but he doesn't know beans about intelligence. He's never even visited his *rezidenturas*. Besides, his people aren't especially motivated, because the FSB gets all the goodies when it comes to budgets and bling. So we really need to know how Tolkachev's network operates."

Boyd paused, then said:

"Just do the best you can."

So that was it. All Malko could do was to approach Zhanna again, without even knowing what he could offer her.

Alexei Khrenkov was taking a hot bath, trying to relax. After leaving Lynn Marsh, he had returned to the Grosvenor Place apartment feeling deeply shaken.

He hadn't checked to see if his Petropavlovsk "guardian angels" had noted his meeting with Lynn Marsh, but it was likely they had. Which meant that they also knew she had seen the CIA agent again. From Moscow's standpoint, her motives didn't matter: she was now "polluted," and Khrenkov was sure to be ordered to break off all contact with her. Moscow, in the person of Rem Tolkachev, wasn't sentimental. As the lord of the swallows, Khrenkov had to be kept away from any possible security breach.

His cell phone, which was on the edge of the bathtub, beeped: an incoming text.

It was very short: *I love you. Lynn.*

Khrenkov stared at it for a long time, feeling torn.

He couldn't believe Lynn had let herself be picked up by another man. She was a straightforward, uncomplicated woman. Linge must have targeted her because he'd learned of Khrenkov's clandestine activity. But from whom? Aside from Tolkachev and Zhanna, no one knew their role in the secret network.

And then it hit him: Zhanna!

She hated Lynn. Could she have approached the CIA agent as a way to make Alexei break up with her?

Khrenkov felt a cold rage rising, but it subsided when a much more serious possibility occurred to him.

Within hours, the Kremlin would know about Lynn's contact with Malko Linge. At which point she would represent a serious security risk in Tolkachev's eyes. And ever since Stalin's time, that kind of problem was always solved the same way, by applying his famous maxim: "No man, no problem."

Lynn Marsh was in mortal danger.

And if Khrenkov tried to intervene, he would automatically come under suspicion himself.

He couldn't imagine abandoning her to her fate. He should at least try to buy her some time. He got out of the tub, dried himself, and carefully typed a text message:

Must return to New York. Will call you as soon as I'm back.

When he pressed "Send," he felt as if he were stabbing himself in the heart. But for the moment it was the only way to shelter the young woman from a danger she didn't even suspect she was facing.

Zhanna's pulse sped up when the spa hostess handed her a sealed envelope in her name, but she waited until she was in the changing room to open it. The message was very short:

We should meet again.

A wave of euphoria washed over her. The CIA had taken the bait! So her idea wasn't as crazy as all that. Now things would get dicey.

Before going into the sauna, she quickly texted Malko:

Be in the barbershop near the spa at 7.

The barbershop was right across the hallway, so she could get to it from the spa without anyone seeing her.

Zhanna had no illusions. She knew she and Alexei were under round-the-clock surveillance. If the Kremlin learned that she'd contacted the CIA agent, Tolkachev would react instantly. And this time, she would be targeted as a potential traitor—not an enviable situation.

Vladimir Krazovsky worked out of a small cubicle at the Petropavlovsk office. On paper, the head of the Khrenkov security detail was listed as an accountant.

A military intelligence and Spetsnaz veteran, Krazovsky had never been outside Russia before this assignment, so he hadn't been identified by any Western security services. A shadowy nationalist who wasn't especially interested in money, he had a visceral hatred for Mikhail Gorbachev, who he felt had dug the Soviet Union's grave.

Krazovsky resigned from the GRU in 1991, but instead of going to work in business like many of his fellows, he applied to the Kremlin administration.

He spent a decade in low-level Kremlin positions before coming to Rem Tolkachev's notice. When the spymaster called him into his little office, the two men quickly discovered how much they had in common. Tolkachev realized he had found a diamond in the rough.

That was the period when the spymaster decided to recruit the Khrenkovs to head the swallows network. He knew he was taking a chance. Alexei was what the Russians call a "legal thief," and his wife, Zhanna, was little better. Tolkachev felt deep contempt for them and their lack of the patriotic fervor that might keep them from temptation. But for now, he needed them.

The spymaster's solution was to build a wall around the pair, to keep them in line. Their cover was perfect in the Americans' eyes, but a slipup could always happen. Which is why he assigned Krazovsky to guard them. His task was to make sure the couple had no contact with anyone suspicious.

Krazovsky worked with a dozen fellow Spetsnaz veterans, some of whom had also never traveled outside Russia. All were given iron-clad "legends"—false identities that would survive investigation—and sent to New York and London in the guise of Petropavlovsk employees. Outside of their surveillance shifts, the men lived very simple lives, with few outside contacts and no friends. Every day, their coded surveillance and observation reports were sent to Moscow, hidden in the steady flow of Petropavlovsk's commercial traffic.

One of the three cell phones in front of Krazovsky rang. It was Gleb Yurchenko, the agent following Malko Linge. He reported that the CIA agent had just entered the Dorchester. Krazovsky noted the time on a sheet in front of him, comparing it to the movements of Zhanna Khrenkov, who had arrived at the Dorchester an hour earlier.

The conclusion was easy to draw, but that wasn't his job. He was just an ordinary *silovik* carrying out a specific mission: keep the swallows program from pollution.

After strolling through the Dorchester gallery as far as the bar, Malko took the elevator to the basement. He passed the entrance to the spa and went down the steps to the barbershop. There were no other customers, and he was greeted with open arms. He had twenty minutes to kill before meeting Zhanna Khrenkov.

"I'd like a shampoo, please," he said.

Feeling upset, Lynn stared at Alexei's text message. When she'd left her lover a few hours earlier, she'd been in seventh heaven. She really was crazy about him. They hadn't made any plans, but she expected that he would soon announce that he was getting divorced.

He phoned several times a day, made love to her all the time, and was forever giving her presents. The most recent one was the gray Mercedes she found parked at her doorstep one morning.

Khrenkov often traveled on short notice, but this sudden trip to New York struck Lynn as odd. Especially since he hadn't phoned. Her intuition told her that something was amiss.

Her dinner with the Austrian prince came to mind. She realized she'd been wrong to hide it from Alexei. But it was only a white lie: she had no designs on her tablemate and had only accepted his dinner invitation for a change of pace after a long day.

Besides, how would Alexei find out? It wasn't as if he were having her followed, after all.

She quickly sent him a text, asking him to call her right away. She had already left a couple of voice mails, but in vain. He wasn't picking up his cell, whereas he usually answered on the first ring when he saw her name displayed.

Lynn buttoned her white lab coat. She had one last patient waiting for her.

She earned a good living, which gave her the independence to only go out with men she liked. And she liked Alexei Khrenkov a lot.

Just the same, she realized she knew very little about him.

Zhanna appeared at the door just as the barber was drying Malko's hair. Catching sight of her in the mirror, he saw her smiling at him ironically.

Leaving a ten-pound tip, he stepped out into the hallway.

"Where are we going?"

"To the mezzanine," she said. "There's never anyone there."

They took the elevator up. Zhanna was right; the mezzanine, with its display cases of luxury goods, was deserted. They sat down on a bench, and she gave him a sharp look.

"So where do we stand?"

"The Agency has checked on Rem Tolkachev, and feels you are sincere. Of course, just the fact that you know who he is doesn't mean you work for him."

"Never mind that," she said, dismissing the objection. "What is your proposal?"

Malko expected the question, but for now could only answer with a bluff.

"We will agree to get rid of Lynn Marsh in exchange for your telling us about the network in the United States."

Malko saw Zhanna's features first tense, then relax. In a low voice, she asked:

"So when are you going to kill the bitch?"

CHAPTER 12

This is where things get sticky, thought Malko.

"There may be a less extreme way to fix your problem that will work just as well," he suggested.

Zhanna Khrenkov visibly stiffened.

"What do you mean?"

She sat there, a solid block of distrust.

"*Dobre*," Malko began, unconsciously shifting to Russian. "Dr. Marsh is very much in love with your husband—or the person she thinks he is, a rich businessman. My idea is very simple: tell her the truth. That not only is Alexei a swindler on the run from the Russian authorities, but he's also a spy. I'm sure she would drop him immediately, as a matter of ethics. And your problem would be solved."

From the look in Zhanna's eyes, he could tell this wasn't a winning tactic. She remained silent for a few moments, then said:

"Even if you're right, why should she believe you?"

"Because the information wouldn't come from me. It could come from a British Home Office representative. A kind of formal heads-up."

"How could you arrange that?"

"The CIA has a very good relationship with British intelligence, and MI5 would be delighted to help roll up a Russian espionage network, even one that doesn't affect them directly."

Zhanna didn't respond, then stood up.

"I don't like the idea, but I'll give it some thought."

"Naturally you'll have to give us some useful information before we get involved," said Malko, standing up in turn. "Assuming you have any, that is."

She whirled on him like a cobra about to strike.

"I know all the dead drops in the United States we use to communicate with the network," she snapped. "And don't get ahead of yourself. I haven't agreed to your suggestion."

She was already at the elevator, apparently not tempted by Malko's offer.

Just the same, he felt he was making progress. At least Zhanna hadn't broken off negotiations.

Gwyneth Robertson was wearing a slightly faded tweed suit, its jacket parted on a mauve satin blouse that allowed her breasts to swing freely. Malko stood to greet her and lightly put his hand on her hip. Under his fingers he could make out the snaking curve of a garter belt. With the beautiful former CIA case officer, all the surprises were good ones.

The waiter had already brought them a bottle of champagne. It was the witching hour, when the Library Bar came to life.

They were seated on a small sofa near the entrance of the second room and could see all the new arrivals. Malko began to relax at last. This strange mission demanded a lot of adrenaline. Partly due to Zhanna Khrenkov's prickly personality, but mainly because of the high stakes in play. He was now convinced that the spy ring in the United States actually existed. If his mission succeeded, it would be the first network to be uncovered since the end of the Cold War, twenty years earlier.

"What are you thinking about?" asked Gwyneth.

"What I plan to do to you later," said Malko with a smile, putting his hand on her tweed skirt and pulling it up a little, baring her thigh. That would hardly shock anyone in that setting. The bar's usual fauna was drifting in: dazzling Eastern European prostitutes with Botox and silicone on draft, wearing outfits so skimpy they proved that less is more. Also a few couples, usually consisting of a very rich toad with a gorgeous woman on his arm, her manners modest only in appearance.

Truth be told, there were few honest women in the bar aside from Gwyneth.

She yawned.

"You can do whatever you like, but you have to feed me first."

"I know a good Japanese place on Half Moon Street: Kiku."

"I said I was hungry!" she said with a pout.

"In that case, how about Alain Ducasse's place at the Dorchester?"

At that, her eyes lit up. She leaned close and ran her tongue lightly over Malko's ear, giving him a tiny, pleasant shiver.

"It'll cost you a fortune," she murmured, "but you won't regret it."

Washed down by a Château Latour 1992, the dinner was a marvel. Ducasse well deserved his reputation. Everything was perfect, from the sautéed foie gras to the lamb with ginger. When she was finished, Gwyneth licked her lips like a satisfied cat.

"The minute I get a raise, I'm coming back here!"

As Malko paid the huge bill—thank you, CIA—she said:

"Want to go do a little dirty dancing to help settle our dinner?"

"What do you have in mind?"

"Let's drop by Peter Stringfellow's Angels, that nasty club in Soho. Some clients introduced me to it. We don't have to spend the whole night there."

"*Vamos!*" said Malko.

In the cab, he couldn't resist slipping his hand under Gwyneth's tweed skirt, moving to the top of her stocking. She squeezed her legs tight.

"Stop it! You know how sensitive I am down there."

Located at the end of Wardour Street, Peter Stringfellow's was nasty indeed. Disco balls hanging from a black ceiling, reddish lighting, widely spaced booths full of men with bar girls, and a small dance floor where couples did the bump and grind. Malko's eye was drawn to a woman in a thigh-high orange dress who was holding her blond chignon in both hands and leaning back, joined to her partner only at the crotch.

A few minutes later, Gwyneth led him onto the floor. It didn't matter what music was playing—everybody danced the same way, holding their partner tight. She began to sway, doing a sexy belly dance, then moved closer, until she was rubbing against him. He grabbed her ass in both hands and pulled her to him.

"Do you want me to make you come?" she asked mischievously.

"Not yet."

She opened her jacket so he could watch her breasts swaying under the satin. As he stroked Gwyneth's nipples in the gloom, Malko felt himself getting caught up in the raw sexual atmosphere. Gwyneth took his hand and said:

"Let's go rent a room!"

"At the Lanesborough?"

"No, we're going to have a quickie on the down low. There's lots of little hotels around here. Kind of hot, don't you think?"

Thirty yards down a side street, a neon sign advertised the Royal Soho Hotel. Gwyneth led the way to the front desk.

"It's fifty pounds, sir," said the sleepy, ill-shaven clerk.

She had already pulled the bills from her purse. Unsurprised, the man handed her a key.

"Number Twenty-Six, young lady. Second floor. Enjoy."

The hallway carpet was threadbare, and the light so dim it felt almost rationed. Their tiny room suggested rationing as well, with its low, narrow bed and greenish night-light. Gwyneth turned around and shrugged off her jacket. Malko was already pinching her nipples. Despite the pain, she unzipped his pants with the skill of a trained nurse. Then she knelt in front of him. Before taking his stiffening cock in her mouth, she gave it an affectionate look and murmured:

"Long time no see."

Malko was so excited, he didn't let her complete the ceremony. He pulled up her tweed skirt, revealing beige stockings and white garters. For once, Gwyneth wasn't wearing panties. When he slipped his fingers inside her, he found that the dirty dancing had excited her as well.

Spinning her around, he made her kneel on the edge of the bed and pushed her skirt above her hips. Anticipating penetration, she arched her back further. The bed was so narrow, her hands were against the wall.

"Fuck me! Fuck me hard!" she cried.

Holding his breath, Malko gently put his cock close to Gwyneth's pussy, but not in it, as she expected. Instead, he set it on her asshole and entered her at full length, as if his cock were being sucked in.

"Son of a bitch!" she squealed, surprised but not displeased.

He withdrew partway, but then plunged in again, drawing a new cry from her. Which didn't make him give up his naughty ways; far from it. Instead, he gripped her hips more firmly.

After a few moments, Malko felt her gradually relax. Gwyneth started giving little moans. Then her hips began to sway, her pelvis rocking back and forth.

Malko came with a yell, matched by a cry from Gwyneth, who had been vigorously caressing herself ever since he first took her.

When he withdrew for good, she stood up, straightened her skirt, and put on her jacket.

"Come on, let's get back to civilization," she said.

These little trips to the dark side were fun, but you didn't want to overdo them.

The man at the front desk didn't even glance up when they walked by ten minutes later. Ten minutes was pretty typical for the couples who frequented his hotel.

After their sordid Soho love nest, the Lanesborough felt like a palace. Gwyneth lay on the big bed sipping champagne, clad only in stockings, garter belt, and high heels.

"By the way, you didn't tell me why you're in London," she said.

Malko gave her the whole story. Gwyneth still had a top-secret clearance, and he didn't hold anything back. But when he described meeting Lynn Marsh at Christie's, she started in surprise.

"I'll be damned! She's my dentist!"

Malko was stunned by the coincidence. With the hun-
dreds of dentists in London, what were the odds that Gwyneth
Robertson would be seeing Lynn Marsh?

"How in the world did that come about?" he asked.

"Lynn's one of the best in the city," she said, "and she shares an
office with a very high-profile guy. And charges accordingly."

"Do you know her well?"

"No, but we've chatted often enough. She doesn't just take care
of your teeth; for some patients, she's like a therapist. She's smart
and good-looking. Are you attracted to her?"

"Sure, but I've only seen her twice. Plus, she seems very much
in love with Alexei Khrenkov. Has she told you anything about her
private life?"

"Not really, except that she's divorced and is seeing someone. I
actually wondered why such a beautiful woman would spend her
time in such an unrewarding line of work."

"Are you due to see her again anytime soon?"

"No, but I can find an excuse to make an appointment if it'll
help you out."

"It might. We'll see."

That was one more string to his bow.

He was now waiting for Zhanna Khrenkov's answer. If she

turned the deal down, the lovely dentist would be of no further interest.

Lynn Marsh was having trouble focusing on the delicate work she was doing on a cracked molar. Her patient was a City banker who constantly flirted with her when he came in. He had already twice invited her to lunch, but she had turned him down. If she started going out with her patients, there'd be no end to it. Besides, she'd been feeling anxious since her last meeting with Alexei.

She'd had no news of him in spite of the many texts she'd sent. She finally confessed to having dinner with Malko Linge, the Austrian prince. She'd been foolish, she said, and hadn't mentioned it for fear of making him angry.

Last night, she even drove along Grosvenor Place, stupidly hoping she might catch a glimpse of him.

She was acting like some lovelorn teenager.

And she couldn't write Alexei a letter, because Zhanna would see it.

Suddenly the pressure got to be too much.

"Please excuse me, I have to step out for a moment," she told her patient. With a bite block propping his jaw open, the banker was in no position to object. Lynn went into her little office, dialed Alexei's number, and left a breathless message:

"I'm begging you, please call me. I miss you so much."

Feeling a little better, she returned to the molar repair.

From the living room, Zhanna heard the apartment door open and close. Alexei had come home, from either his bank or his girlfriend. Zhanna willed herself not to move. There were times when she wanted to kill him, too. He was sure to stroll in acting as if everything were normal.

She waited for a while, but Alexei didn't come in, and she eventually went into his bedroom. His clothes were strewn on the floor, and the bathroom door was closed. Zhanna stopped, intrigued. Alexei had been acting oddly for the last couple of days. He was more taciturn than usual, and seemed upset.

She had asked him if there was a problem with Moscow, and he had said no.

A little too quickly.

Spotting his jacket on the floor, she suddenly got an idea. She took his cell phone from the pocket and ran to the walk-in closet. Turning it on, she keyed in the voice-mail access code. There were thirteen messages. When she heard the most recent one, she nearly dropped the phone: it was Lynn Marsh! The woman sounded almost unrecognizable. In a hoarse, broken voice, she begged Alexei to call her back.

Zhanna listened to three more similar messages, then quickly returned the phone to Alexei's jacket.

Back in the living room, she lit herself a Pall Mall, feeling shaken and perplexed. What troubled her even more than Alexei's infidelity was Lynn Marsh's connection to Malko Linge. She hadn't expected that. The CIA agent's interest in Marsh might be purely professional, of course. It just showed that he wasn't putting all his eggs in one basket.

But it weakened Zhanna's position vis-à-vis the Agency, because she didn't know what Alexei might have told her. Zhanna was prepared to take chances, but something troubled her: from Marsh's tone, it sounded as if her husband had broken up with her.

Which meant her problem was solved.

Only she had to be sure that this wasn't just a temporary split.

And for that she would have to interrogate her husband—very gingerly.

She had to know why Alexei was leaving a woman he loved.

Malko and Gwyneth had just reached the front doors of the Lanesborough when he received a call from an unidentified number on his cell.

"Malko, it's Irving," said a man's voice. "I hope you weren't asleep."

It was the CIA's head of counterintelligence. What could he want with Malko at midnight? But then he remembered it was only seven p.m. in Washington.

"Not at all," he said. "What can I do for you?"

"I'd like us to have breakfast together tomorrow."

Malko thought he hadn't heard right.

"In Washington?"

"No, in London. At Grosvenor Square. I'm at Dulles, and my flight leaves in forty minutes."

"No problem," said Malko. "Have a good trip."

He was mystified. Why would Boyd fly to London a second time, when Malko and Zhanna hadn't yet reached a deal?

Aside from the guards, Rem Tolkachev was almost certainly the only person in the Kremlin to be working so late. It was two o'clock in the morning, but the spymaster wanted to fully absorb the evening's reports from London.

And reach a decision.

The latest news was bad.

The CIA was starting to sniff around the Khrenkovs. Alexei

hadn't been "polluted," but Malko Linge was now in direct and regular contact with Zhanna Khrenkov and Alexei's girlfriend.

Those were the facts.

What did Linge know, and how had he found the Khrenkovs? Was there a leak in the network? Had one of the swallows been turned and fingered Alexei Khrenkov?

Because of the dead-letter system, that wasn't likely. But each of the swallows had met Khrenkov at least once, at the very beginning.

Tolkachev was strongly tempted to order the couple back to Russia posthaste, so as to break off any dangerous connections. But that entailed a number of inconvenient consequences.

First, the Khrenkovs would be burned. The moment the Americans saw them returning to Russia, where they were in trouble with the law, they would get suspicious.

Second, the network would lose its head. Tolkachev would have to find a replacement for the couple, which wouldn't be easy.

Finally, if the Khrenkovs really didn't know anything about the source of the pollution—even after being interrogated in Lefortovo—Tolkachev would be back where he started.

It would be impossible to restart the network without knowing what was going on. And that would mean throwing away years of hard work.

Suddenly another solution occurred to him. It was risky, tough to initiate, and difficult to execute. But it was the only way to answer all his questions.

After thinking for a moment, he carefully set down his cup of sweetened tea, left the office, and went to retrieve his Lada from the garage. He would give himself until tomorrow to put his plan into effect.

Irving Boyd looked much fresher than he had on his last visit to London. On the small table in the conference room next to his office, Richard Spicer had set out toast, Danish pastries, and croissants along with tea and coffee, but the counterintelligence chief wasn't hungry. After a quick swig of coffee, he pulled a file from his briefcase and gave Malko an admiring look.

"You have no idea how much excitement your Russian spy ring has generated in Washington."

"Come on," said Malko. "I don't think the security of the nation is at risk. The network may be a nuisance, but it's not like they're stealing the atomic bomb."

Boyd smilingly brushed the demurrer aside.

"True enough. Even the FBI, which missed the network because they're so focused on Islamic terrorism, feels they probably aren't very high-level spies. But there's a lot more to the picture."

Boyd leaned closer over the table, accidentally brushing against the croissants.

"We absolutely have to arrest the members of the network. That's an order straight from the White House."

"Because President Obama needs a success before the midterm elections?" asked Malko with a smile.

"No, it's more important than that."

Boyd put on his glasses and opened the file in front of him.

"Here's the deal. Four of our people have been sitting in Russian prisons for years. We want to get them out.

"The first is a very well-known scientist named Igor Sutyagin. We approached him during an international conference on nuclear proliferation. He's an expert in miniaturization, an area where we need to know how our Russian friends are doing.

"In 2004, Sutyagin was sentenced to hard labor in Camp Fifteen in Siberia. He wrote his family recently that he can't hang on much longer. We were careless with him. We thought the FSB had slacked off, and we didn't take all the security precautions we could have.

"The second man is Alexander Zaporozhsky, who was a member of the First Directorate back in Shebarshin's time. He started working for us in 1987, when he was stationed in China. His mistake was to continue after returning to Moscow. He's been in prison since 2003, but we don't know where. He spent a year in Lefortovo under terrible conditions. They blanketed the floor of his cell with large salt crystals, and let him nearly die of thirst. A bank account with more than six hundred thousand dollars is waiting for him in Washington.

"The third is Sergei Skripal, a KGB colonel who transferred to military intelligence. He was careless, too. He walked right into the American embassy, not realizing that the FSB had been watching him for months. Normally, someone in that situation would never get out of the Lubyanka alive. But Skripal was lucky. He confessed, so they let him off with thirteen years of hard labor in the camps. His wife died of cancer, and his son managed to emigrate, so he's completely alone in Russia."

Boyd recited these dismaying facts in a monotone.

"Is that it?" asked Malko soberly.

"No, it isn't. The fourth one is Gennady Vasilenko, a man the Agency would give anything to get back. He's done incredible work for us since 1978. He was recruited in Washington and gave us valuable information until Robert Hanssen betrayed him to the KGB.

"Vasilenko was arrested in 1983 and sent to Lefortovo, charged with espionage. Before they could shoot him, they needed his signature on a confession. But he never admitted anything and never signed the confession. In 1983 they struck him from the KGB rolls, canceled his pension, and threw him out on the street.

"He survived until 1990, only getting a job after the Soviet Union collapsed. And then he started working for us again, in 1995. But this time the FSB was suspicious. They nailed him in 2005 and sent him to Lefortovo. To make up for missing him the first time, the Russians decided they weren't about to let him go. He was given eighteen years and is leaving for Siberia soon."

Boyd paused.

"For the Agency, getting these men back is a sacred mission. Word is passed from each director to the next. Thanks to you, we now have a chance of freeing four people who have done great service for the United States."

"I don't see how," Malko admitted.

"It's pretty obvious," Boyd said with a smile. "If we're able to bust the Khrenkov network agents, we'll have two options.

"Option one: we try them and send them to jail for years. Make an example of them to demonstrate the duplicity of the Russians who pretend to make nice while spying on us. That would make the White House look good, of course.

"Option two is much smarter. We discreetly arrest the network people, and make the Russians an offer: their spies for our spies. That way, they save face and we get our people back. What do you think?"

Malko could almost feel the years falling away. He was back in the Cold War, when such exchanges were made on the Glienicke Bridge, the ugly metal span between West Berlin and Potsdam in East Germany known as the "bridge of spies."

Boyd's idea was attractive, but there were a few hitches.

A lot of hitches, actually.

"Aren't you counting your chickens before they're hatched, Irving?" he asked. "Right now, we don't know where those spies are. I'm not sure I can convince Zhanna Khrenkov to cooperate— assuming she's able to, because she might still be bluffing. Even if we solve that problem, nothing says the Russians will agree to a swap."

"That's true, but we have to act as if they will," said Boyd. "Your mission has absolute priority. You have a free hand to do whatever it takes to convince her. You can even offer her a carrot. Tell her that if she delivers the network, we'll extend protection and immunity to her and her husband. They're already rich, so the future will be wide open."

Malko had his doubts.

"You seem to forget that the FSB has a long arm," he said. "Remember Alexander Litvinenko."

"We'll do everything in our power to protect them," said Boyd doggedly.

In other words, reserve two spaces in Arlington National Cemetery for a pair of deserving traitors.

"I have to leave this evening," Boyd continued. "Do you have any questions?"

"No, but a lot of work. For starters, I'm going to take a calculated risk, even though it weakens my position. I'm going to contact Zhanna to see if she has thought the matter over."

For once, Tolkachev was late in getting to his office. He had stopped at the Yeliseyevsky store to pick up some red caviar he'd ordered.

He drafted a short memo for his superior, explaining the plan he had in mind.

For a foreign operation, especially one that entailed political risks, Tolkachev didn't want to act alone. While waiting for an answer, he sipped sweet tea and smoked one of his pastel-colored cigarettes.

The red light over his door came on; he had a visitor. Tolkachev stood up and went to the door. Without a word, a man in a gray suit handed him an envelope, saluted, and left. Tolkachev waited until he was seated at his desk to open it.

The envelope contained the note he had sent two hours earlier. Handwritten in the margin was a single word, *Da*, followed by Vladimir Putin's familiar signature.

Tolkachev just had been given a green light to kidnap the CIA agent and make him reveal why he had taken an interest in the Khrenkovs.

Only when that was done would Tolkachev consider his next step.

CHAPTER

14

"**There's a covered arcade that runs between Jermyn** Street and Piccadilly," said Zhanna. "One of the shops sells small stone carvings. I'll be there around noon, but I won't have much time."

She hung up without waiting for Malko's reply.

He had called Zhanna on Irving Boyd's instructions, though he was reluctant to approach her again so soon. He was still at Grosvenor Square, so at least he could walk to the meeting. And it wasn't raining, thank God.

As he headed down Piccadilly he silently prayed that she would deliver the goods.

He reached the arcade at five past twelve, and spotted a store with carved animals in the window. Inside he could see Zhanna chatting with a mustachioed sales clerk who was holding a beautiful onyx rhinoceros. She glanced at Malko briefly, then resumed her conversation with the clerk. Malko moved to the next window, waiting for her to come out of the shop.

Five minutes later, Zhanna emerged carrying a large package. She was wearing sunglasses, which he'd never seen on her before.

"Do you have time for a drink?" he asked.

"No, I don't," she said flatly. "I suppose you've come for my answer."

"That's right."

"If you hadn't phoned, I would've called to tell you to stop bothering me. Forget this whole business. I made up the whole story."

"All of it?" he asked in disbelief. "Even the existence of Lynn Marsh?"

"That doesn't matter," she said, dismissing the young dentist. "Don't try to make trouble for me and my husband. If the police question me, I'll tell them I invented it whole cloth."

With a crisp "*Dasvidanya*," she turned on her heels and walked toward Jermyn Street, leaving Malko slack-jawed.

Irving Boyd's dream of a spy swap was going up in smoke.

Malko walked to Piccadilly and hailed a taxi across from Le Meridien.

"Grosvenor Square, please," he told the cabbie.

No point in making Richard Spicer wait to hear the good news.

Zhanna Khrenkov felt wonderful. She'd had a long conversation with Alexei that morning. He told her he had broken up with the Marsh woman and swore he would never see her again. He even suggested that the two of them take a trip to the Seychelles together.

It would be like a second honeymoon.

If she hadn't heard Lynn Marsh's messages on his phone, she might not have believed him. But they fit perfectly with what he had told her.

Besides the joy she felt at getting rid of her hated rival, Zhanna was relieved not to have to betray the *lastochkas* network to the Americans. She had chosen to ignore the risk she would face at their Kremlin masters' hands, but deep down she knew that she would have exposed herself and her husband to tremendous danger.

All's well that ends well, she thought. Rem Tolkachev would never know about her machinations, and she and Alexei could get on with their life of carefree luxury.

The CIA station chief was in shock.

"What do you think is behind her turnaround?"

Malko shrugged.

"There could be lots of reasons," he said. "Maybe Alexei found out about his wife's plans and convinced her they would lead to disaster. Or Lynn Marsh decided to break it off on her own, for some reason. It could be anything. But in any case, there's nothing left for me but to fly back to Austria."

"If you don't mind, I'd like you to give Irving the news in person," said Spicer. "He'll be here at five o'clock."

The CIA counterintelligence chief couldn't hide his dismay.

"This is a real kick in the teeth!" he said. "Langley's going to be disappointed. And our Russian friends will go on rotting in prison."

"I did everything I could," said Malko. "As I said, Zhanna Khrenkov is a tough nut to crack. I won't be able to change her mind."

"Do you think she really made it all up?"

"Certainly not," he said. "But there is one thing you can do: give the Khrenkovs' names to the FBI. They might get something on them."

Boyd sighed.

"The damned FBI never finds anything, unless it's part of

some scheme they cooked up themselves. I'll tell the Bureau about the Khrenkovs, of course, but they're sure to keep their noses clean now. We can't even deport Zhanna; she's American."

"I'm really sorry, Irving," said Malko. "But we sometimes strike out in this business, as you well know. Maybe it was too good to be true."

Malko felt bitter too. He'd wound up believing the beautiful story about an exchange of spies. And thinking of the agents locked away in prisons or labor camps for years on end made him heartsick.

"Okay," said Boyd with a sigh. "I'm going to the airport."

"Mind dropping me off at the Lanesborough?" asked Malko.

Feeling depressed, all he wanted now was to get out of London. He decided to cancel his dinner date with Gwyneth and stay at the hotel until his flight to Vienna.

It was nearly midnight, but the Lanesborough was still hopping, what with people returning from the theater and others drinking in the bar. A gorgeous black call girl headed for the elevators with a bearded man who barely reached to her shoulder. The desk clerk modestly averted his gaze, taking a sudden interest in the room register.

At the Lanesborough, the customer was king.

Nor did the clerk pay much attention when he saw two men come out of the bar a few minutes later and walk to the elevators. One of them had a large attaché case; the other, a black leather bag of the kind that doctors carry.

Having downed half a dozen shots of vodka, Malko collapsed full length on his bed. He hated failure, and even though it wasn't his fault, he would be going back to Austria with a bitter taste in his mouth.

The two men that the front desk clerk had vaguely noticed stopped in front of Room 227. The hallway led to only four rooms and ended in a cul-de-sac. It was deserted.

One of the men went to stand at the end of the hall, watching the elevators. The other set his attaché case down on the thick carpet. Opening it revealed a metal tank that took up almost all the space. Attached to it was a rubber tube that ended in a black suction cup.

The man took the tube from the case and firmly stuck the suction cup over the door's key slot. Then he turned a valve on the tank. A slight hiss was heard, and the tube stiffened under the pressure of a gas. The man checked his watch. He needed two minutes; not a lot, but a very long time under the circumstances. If someone showed up, he would have to start over again.

Luckily, no one appeared.

When the two minutes were up, he peeled off the suction cup, coiled the tube, and closed the case. He headed to the elevator without a word for his partner, who simply nodded.

After the man with the attaché case went downstairs, his partner waited five minutes, then took a magnetic card and slid it into the door lock. It took a few tries, but a green light eventually blinked on and the lock clicked open.

The hardest part was over.

He opened the door partway and switched on the lights. Seeing a man asleep on the bed, he quickly threw open the window, then went back out to the hallway, leaving the door ajar. He dialed a number on his cell, spoke a few words, and returned to his position at the end of the hallway.

———

Because Malko had canceled their date, Gwyneth agreed to have dinner with her think-tank colleagues. The evening turned out to be deadly dull, and long.

She finally got free a little past midnight and thought of giving Malko a call. They could have a drink at the Library, or do something more if the mood was right.

Gwyneth got his voice mail almost immediately. A bit surprised that he'd already gone to sleep, she left him a short message.

The black ambulance with the blue light bar pulled up in front of the Lanesborough. Two burly paramedics in white coats walked around to the back and rolled out a gurney. A third man, wearing a cap, remained behind the wheel.

To the bowler-hatted doorman who gave them an inquiring look, one of the paramedics said:

"One of your guests is sick, apparently."

"You can go see the front desk."

The two EMTs crossed the lobby and spoke to the clerk.

"We just got a call for Room 227. One of your guests has fallen ill. A doctor is already up with him."

This was news to the desk clerk, but he didn't take it amiss. The guest very likely called the doctor himself. As the two men headed for the elevator, the clerk turned his attention to an Italian couple who were insisting that they had a reservation.

When the two paramedics reached the hallway to Room 227, the man who had picked the door lock stepped aside to let them in.

Pulling the gurney next to the bed, they deftly rolled the sleeping man onto it. In moments, they had him secured and covered with a blanket, held down with leather straps to keep him from falling.

Meanwhile, the third man closed the window, made sure they hadn't forgotten anything, and picked up his black bag. Then he went out, closed the door, and hung a "Do Not Disturb" sign on the doorknob.

When the two men rolled their gurney across the lobby past the front desk, the man carrying the black bag gave the clerk a polite nod. With his case and serious expression, he looked very much like a doctor.

The two nurses rolled the gurney into the back of the ambulance and climbed in along with the "doctor." The ambulance slowly headed out toward Grosvenor Place.

Gwyneth Robertson hadn't slept well. She looked at her clock: it was nine thirty. She called Malko again, surprised that he hadn't called back. It went directly to voice mail. She then tried his room at the Lanesborough but got the hotel answering service.

That's strange, she thought. Malko was usually very good about returning calls.

Gwyneth called the front desk and asked to speak to him. This time she had a little more success.

"I think Mr. Linge got sick last night," said the desk clerk, who sounded busy. "The night clerk said that an ambulance came for him."

"An ambulance? Where did they take him?"

"I don't know, ma'am, I wasn't on duty. Would you like me to find out?"

"No, thanks."

Now worried, Gwyneth quickly got dressed and ran out to her

Mini. By the time she pulled up at the Lanesborough, her pulse was racing. Without stopping at the front desk, she hurried up to the second floor. Everything looked normal, but she spotted the "Do Not Disturb" sign on Room 227. Back downstairs, she demanded that someone accompany her up to the room. With ill grace, the desk clerk agreed.

At the door to the room, Gwyneth pointed at the sign:

"Doesn't that strike you as odd? If Mr. Linge was taken to a hospital, who could have hung out the sign? Open the door, please."

Now thoroughly cowed, the clerk did so.

The room was empty, and the bed unmade. Gwyneth immediately noticed a strange smell in the air. Now feeling deeply concerned, she took out her cell and called Richard Spicer.

The station chief was delighted to hear her voice.

"Gwyneth, what a pleasant surprise!"

"I'm not sure the surprise is a good one," said the former case officer. "When did you last talk to Malko?"

"Yesterday, early evening. A friend dropped him off at the Lanesborough. Why?"

"Was he feeling all right?"

"Sure."

"In that case you better get over here to the hotel. I think Malko may have been kidnapped."

CHAPTER
15

Malko had to strain to breathe through his nose, but he
didn't have any choice: thick tape was plastered across his mouth,
right up to his ears. He'd regained consciousness some time earlier to find himself in complete darkness, strapped to a bed. He
was wearing only his underpants, as he had been when he'd gone
to sleep.

There was no way to know what had happened. He had a sour
taste in his mouth and a dull, persistent headache. He felt slightly
nauseated.

Though it seemed incredible, he'd obviously been drugged
and kidnapped from his room at the Lanesborough. How had
they gotten him out of the hotel? He couldn't remember anything
about it.

Gradually, his brain began to work again. Why this strange
kidnapping, and what did the kidnappers want from him? It had
to be connected to the Khrenkov affair, but the timing made no
sense, since he'd just abandoned his mission.

Foreign intelligence services seem to be treating London like
their own private war zone, he reflected.

Malko tried to move, but without success: his bonds were
so tight, he could barely raise his hips, which didn't do much
good.

His eyes were also taped shut, and he had no idea where he was, or any notion of how long he'd been held prisoner.

Just then, he heard the sound of a door being unlocked. From the muffled noises, he gathered that one or more people had entered the room. Almost immediately, the straps securing his left arm to the bed railing were loosened. He felt a chill on the inside of his elbow, which was being swabbed with damp cotton. A vaguely medicinal smell reached his nostrils, and he felt a slight stab of pain. He was being given an intravenous injection, and he could feel something flowing into his vein.

What were they giving him? Fighting a rising sense of panic, he told himself that if they'd wanted to poison him, they could've done it in his room at the Lanesborough.

The injection seemed to go on and on. Gradually Malko's head began to feel heavy, and he had trouble thinking clearly. When they finally pulled the needle out, he barely felt it.

They carefully strapped his arm back to the railing. Now semiconscious, Malko realized he was alone again. But he was floating in a kind of pleasant haze that eased his anxiety. He felt almost good and lost consciousness without realizing it.

The Lanesborough general manager felt so mortified, he wanted the polished floor beneath his feet to open up and swallow him. Never in his wildest dreams would he have expected to find himself interrogated like a criminal by a senior MI5 official.

Yet Sir William Wolseley showed him only the most exquisite politeness. He was just curious to know, he said, how unknown people could have drugged and kidnapped a Lanesborough guest without anyone noticing.

"Of course I questioned everybody on duty last night," the

manager said. "The front desk saw two paramedics and a doctor leave with a guest who had fallen ill."

"And nobody thought to talk to them?"

"No, they didn't," said the manager unhappily. "Nothing like this has ever happened before. I assure you that—"

"Very well," said the MI5 official, cutting him off.

Wolseley understood there was nothing more to be learned here. It was a classic case of negligence.

To Richard Spicer, who had followed the conversation in silence, he said:

"Let's go upstairs to see how the examination of the room is getting on."

The Lanesborough was crawling with MI5 and Special Branch agents. After Gwyneth Robertson sounded the alarm, they descended on the hotel, calling in every staffer on night duty for questioning, and examining the concierge and front-desk guest registers.

So far, in vain.

Assisted by a police forensic specialist, a Special Branch team was going through Malko's room with a fine-tooth comb.

The officer in charge came over to Wolseley.

"We think we know how the kidnappers did it, Sir William. A powerful soporific gas was pumped in through the keyhole of the door. We've collected traces of it, and we'll analyze them, but I wouldn't expect any big surprises. They opened the door with a magnetic passkey. The person in the room was unconscious by then, and a second team carried him out, disguised as paramedics."

"What about their vehicle?" asked Spicer.

"A black ambulance with a blue light bar. No logo or lettering. And nobody thought to write down the license number, of course."

An appalled hush fell over the group.

With so little to go on, they weren't likely to find the kidnappers any time soon.

Wolseley turned to Spicer.

"Let's all meet at Thames House, Richard, and see where we stand."

The CIA station chief hadn't yet alerted Washington, partly because he didn't have any specifics, partly because of the time difference. But he couldn't put it off any longer.

The man conducting the interrogation watched his subject's eyes carefully. Though his blindfold had been removed, Malko had the bizarre sensation of being two people at once, as if he could observe himself.

Electrodes had been stuck to various parts of his body and temples and connected to a machine that looked like a lie detector. The person asking the questions studied the erratically moving needles on three dials.

It was all being recorded, of course.

To remove a possible psychological barrier, the man was interrogating Malko in German.

In a slow, patient voice, he asked:

"*Also, fing alles in Monte-Carlo an, nicht wahr?*"

"*Jawohl,*" said Malko, in a strangely dull tone. "It all started in Monte Carlo."

The interrogation had begun. Malko hadn't noticed that they'd set an IV catheter on the back of his left hand to maintain a constant level of the drug in his blood. They were using a substance like sodium thiopental that reduced his psychological defenses while stimulating his memories. Later, when he woke up and the drug was flushed from his system, he wouldn't remember anything about the episode, even though it had gone deeply into his memory.

The Russians, whose research on chemistry and poisons was always on the cutting edge, had developed a perfect truth serum. It wasn't available commercially, of course, and the intelligence services used it only under carefully controlled conditions.

The interrogator asked his next question in the same monotonous voice, as if talking to someone who was hypnotized. He figured that within two hours at the most, he would have plumbed his subject's memory.

The interrogator was exceptionally skilled at his work, which is why he'd been specially flown in from Moscow the night before. He traveled on an expertly forged Dutch passport, seemingly coming from Greece. British immigration hadn't noticed anything amiss.

When his job here was done, the man would fly back to Moscow with the recording of the interrogations, surrender the passport, and return to his regular job in the Krasny Bogatir poisons laboratory.

"Richard, why didn't you tell us that Malko Linge was here on a risky assignment?" asked Wolseley reproachfully. "We could have put one of our A4 teams on him. That saved his life once before, you'll recall."

"We had no idea he was in danger, Sir William," said Spicer. "It was a routine background investigation on a matter that didn't concern Great Britain."

"Still, he was kidnapped here in London."

The meeting was being held on the fourth floor of Thames

House. In addition to the MI5 and CIA men, it included the head of British counterintelligence's Russian section, and a Special Branch representative.

"We absolutely have to find him!" said Spicer. "I'm sure his life is in danger."

"Given what we have to go on, that's going to be difficult," said Wolseley, looking discouraged. "No descriptions, nothing about the ambulance, and even less about its destination. Prince Linge could be anywhere."

He turned to the Russian counterintelligence specialist.

"What do you think, John?"

"I was notified two hours ago and immediately increased surveillance around the FSB *rezidentura* and the SVR office in Kensington," said the man, "but we didn't see anything unusual. I also talked to Cheltenham, and they haven't noticed any recent spikes in communications traffic. Naturally, we're going to keep a close eye on the agents we've identified in the past, but that's about all we can do."

The Special Branch representative spoke up:

"We've alerted the airports and all the country's exit points. I'm having the area ambulance companies questioned, to see if someone rented or stole one of their vehicles. We won't hear anything for a couple of hours at least, and I wouldn't count on that too much anyway."

Feeling increasingly gloomy, Spicer started when Wolseley spoke to him.

"Richard, would you like us to apply for a search warrant for the Khrenkov flat? It's already under permanent surveillance."

The CIA station chief had been forced to share his little family secret with the British, so the cousins now knew all about Malko's assignment.

Spicer thought for a moment, then said:

"That can wait, since you're already watching them."

Wolseley made a show of looking at his watch.

"Then I don't think we have anything else to discuss for now. Naturally I'll let you know if I hear anything new. I'm personally very fond of Prince Linge and I wouldn't want . . ."

He let the sentence trail off.

They shook hands in silence. It made Spicer sick to know that his kidnapped operative was being held somewhere in London and there wasn't a thing he could do about it.

"I'm heading to Grosvenor Square," he said. "I have a briefing scheduled." The station chief had asked Gwyneth Robertson to come aboard, to help him understand what might have happened. The former case officer had dropped her usual carefree manner and was chain-smoking Dunhills, right under a sign that specifically prohibited it.

"I should have trusted my gut!" said Gwyneth bitterly. "I felt like seeing him last night after dinner, but I didn't want to bother him. If I'd gone there, maybe this shit wouldn't have happened!"

Spicer raised his hands in an appeasing gesture.

"Don't beat yourself up, Gwyneth. What I want to understand is: Who kidnapped him and why?"

"Who? The Russians, of course."

"Because they found out we had suspicions about the Khrenkovs?"

"Seems pretty obvious, don't you think?"

"But Malko had wrapped up his mission. Zhanna turned him down, so the project was dead in the water. We'd have stayed on the Khrenkovs, of course, but as part of a long-term investigation that didn't involve Malko. Nobody had any reason to put him out of commission."

"That might not have been the idea," she said. "If they wanted to kill him, it would've been easy to do it in his bed last night."

"So why kidnap him?"

"Maybe he found something out. . . ." The ex–CIA case officer sounded uncertain.

"He would've told me," said Spicer.

A hush descended on the two. They were at a loss.

Gwyneth lit another Dunhill and thoughtfully blew out a plume of smoke.

"I have an idea!" she said suddenly. "There's no point in questioning the Khrenkovs; they'll just clam up. But we still have Lynn Marsh."

"Alexei's girlfriend?"

"That's right. As it happens, I know her. If I can talk to her, we might be able to understand what happened."

Gwyneth quickly explained how she knew the dentist, which came as a total surprise to Spicer.

"That's a good idea," he said. "But you'll have to tell her the truth. And as far as we know, Alexei Khrenkov isn't aware that we suspect him. Aren't you afraid Marsh will turn around and tell him everything?"

"That's a risk," she said, "but if we want to get Malko back, we better take it."

"So you're going to tell Marsh exactly who Khrenkov really is?"

"I don't see any other way."

"In that case, you've got carte blanche," said the station chief. "Let's keep our fingers crossed."

CHAPTER

16

Lynn Marsh flashed her usual bright smile as she wel-comed Gwyneth Robertson into her office. With the contrast between her white coat and her long, black-stockinged legs, the young dentist looked very attractive.

"You were lucky a cancellation opened up," she said. "What can I do for you today?"

"My teeth are fine, Lynn. I needed to see you for another reason. And it's urgent."

"Really? What's that?"

The two women had never discussed personal matters, and the dentist was a little taken aback.

"I've never talked much about my life," said Gwyneth, "but I have to tell you that I spent fifteen years working for the CIA."

Lynn was now quite puzzled.

"What does that have to do with your being here today?"

"A lot, actually. And I suggest you sit down, because you might find what I'm about to say upsetting."

Mystified, the dentist sat in her desk chair.

"You're seeing a man called Alexei Khrenkov," Gwyneth began.

Lynn started.

"How do you know about that? And what business is it of yours?"

Unruffled, the former CIA case officer continued.

"Mr. Khrenkov is Russian, as you know. What you don't know is that he and his wife are fugitives from Russian justice. They fled the country after embezzling seven hundred million dollars. But that's not why I'm here today. The reason I'm here is that Mr. Khrenkov is also suspected of running a spy ring in the United States."

The blood had drained from the dentist's face. Her throat was so tight, she wasn't able to say a word.

Gwyneth proceeded to tell her the whole story, including Malko's alarming kidnapping the night before. Lynn seemed stunned, overwhelmed.

Gwyneth waited for some color to come back to her face, then asked:

"Were you aware of what I've just told you?"

"No, of course not," she said in a dull voice, shaking her head. "But—"

"Do you believe me?"

"Yes, but—"

"If you have any doubts, I can take you to MI5 headquarters, where they'll confirm my story."

Lynn Marsh shook her head again and roused herself.

"I don't need that. But why did you come to tell me all this? It doesn't concern me anymore."

"It doesn't? Why not?"

"Because Alexei broke up with me a few days ago. I haven't had any word from him since."

To the former case officer, this came as news.

"Did he say why?"

"No, and he didn't even send me a text to explain himself. Nothing; just silence. But I didn't know anything about the stuff you just told me, so it couldn't have been for that."

Now it was Gwyneth's turn to be astonished. Khrenkov had ended his relationship with Marsh. So that's why Zhanna broke off contact with the CIA. She was rid of her rival and no longer had any reason to give up the network.

Coming here sure wasn't a waste of my time, thought Gwyneth to herself, even though the breakup didn't explain Malko's kidnapping. Aloud, she asked:

"What do you plan to do?"

"Nothing. Try to forget him."

"We think that Mr. Khrenkov doesn't know we suspect him," said Gwyneth. "If he finds out, it might have pretty serious consequences. We're still hoping to arrest him."

"He won't learn about it from me," said Lynn, her voice now stronger.

"Do you have any idea what happened to Malko Linge?"

The dentist stared at her.

"How could I? I barely know the man. I've only seen him twice in my life, and I had no idea who he was. I thought he was just a playboy who wanted to get me into bed."

That's actually not far from the truth, Gwyneth thought wryly. Then she looked at her watch and said:

"I think I've told you everything. Do you want protection?"

"Protection?" The dentist was surprised. "Whatever for?"

"We don't know the whole story yet. You've been in close contact with Alexei Khrenkov. As long as we don't know why Mr. Linge was kidnapped, we have to be careful."

She handed Lynn her business card.

"If you notice anything unusual, call me. Otherwise, don't hesitate to call nine-nine-nine. I expect I'll see you again soon."

Lynn walked the former CIA agent out to the landing. Then she returned to the office, sank into her chair, and burst into tears. It was too much for one day. Learning that your lover is a crook and you're surrounded by spies is more than most people can handle.

Feeling unable to go poking around in yet another mouth, Lynn told her assistant to cancel her next patient.

"It doesn't make any sense!" said Spicer. "They had no reason to attack him."

Gwyneth was sitting in a deep leather armchair across from the station chief's desk. She shook her head.

"We don't know the whole story," she said, "but let's see what we do know. First, Malko is approached in Monte Carlo by Zhanna Khrenkov, who offers him a weird deal: she'll reveal a sleeper Russian spy network in the United States if the CIA kills her husband's girlfriend.

"Malko investigates and finds that most of what Zhanna said checks out. The girlfriend exists—that's Lynn Marsh—and Zhanna knows the name of a very important Russian spymaster. Then, at their last meeting, she tells Malko the deal is off."

The station chief picked up the thread.

"Thanks to you, we now know why," he said. "Alexei spontaneously breaks up with his girlfriend, so Zhanna's problem is taken care of."

Gwyneth smiled slightly.

"I don't believe in 'spontaneously,' Richard. A man doesn't break up with a woman he's crazy about without a very good reason. I think someone from the outside pressured him into it."

"Like who?"

"I'm not sure, but whoever created the network and put Khrenkov in charge must still be watching over it. The Russians have always been very cautious. I imagine the Khrenkovs are under close surveillance. To my way of thinking, that's where we should look. The people watching the Khrenkovs probably felt Malko was getting too close to the pot of gold and went into action."

"I can understand their wanting to get rid of Malko," said Spicer, "but why make Alexei dump his girlfriend? She wasn't involved in any of his secret activities."

Gwyneth lit herself a fresh Dunhill and said:

"If we assume the Khrenkovs were under surveillance, the Russians would extend that surveillance to Lynn Marsh the moment she got intimate with Alexei. We know Malko met Marsh twice. Maybe the Russians figured he had targeted her and was trying to get information about the network. In that case, Moscow Central would order Khrenkov to leave her. An order he couldn't disobey since the Russians have him by the short hairs."

Spicer nodded at her analysis.

"I can buy all that, but it still doesn't explain why they would take such a big risk in kidnapping Malko."

"There, you've got me."

Silence fell on the CIA office, eventually broken by Gwyneth.

"Do you have any news from MI5?"

Spicer shrugged.

"They don't have any evidence, so I don't expect much from them. Remember the Litvinenko affair. The FSB or some other agency killed the guy right under the Brits' noses, and it took them weeks to figure out how it was done."

"What if the two operations were run by the same person?" asked Gwyneth. "Think of it, Richard. They used the same methods, and both required a lot of people and logistics to be carried out. I doubt Malko's kidnapping was done by the local *rezidentura*. They probably didn't even know about it."

"That's not a bad thought," said the CIA station chief. "And Zhanna Khrenkov did finger Rem Tolkachev, and by extension the Kremlin. In the Litvinenko affair we were always convinced that the orders came from the Kremlin, and that's where Tolkachev hangs his hat."

Gwyneth tensely stubbed out the Dunhill she had just lit.

"So what are you doing to get Malko back? Do you plan to lean on the Khrenkovs?"

Spicer shook his head.

"I doubt they're in the loop. And there's nothing we—"

The young woman interrupted him.

"Do you think he's already dead?"

"I didn't mean to say that," protested Spicer. "But it's not looking good."

"In that case, we better start praying."

In his darkened world, Malko had lost track of time. Every so often, someone removed his gag and gave him a drink or a piece of chocolate, but he never saw the person.

Malko was again thinking clearly, though he couldn't remember exactly what had happened. He also had no idea why he was being held prisoner.

No one had threatened him, or even spoken to him. He didn't know where he was and, especially, what lay ahead. As long as he was still alive, there was hope. He trusted the CIA and the cousins to do everything in their power to get him out of there. The question was, could they?

Fatigue again overwhelmed him, and he fell asleep.

Feeling gratified, Rem Tolkachev closed the file containing the transcript of the Malko Linge thiopental interrogation. He now knew exactly what had happened. There was just one person to blame. Well, one and a half persons.

Once again, Tolkachev's method had worked: knowing all the ins and outs before taking action.

He now faced two equally significant decisions.

First, what to do with the Khrenkovs. After this, the couple would be carefully tracked by the Americans and the British. They were burned, and would forever be suspect, even if they stopped all their espionage activities.

And there was an additional risk, about which Tolkachev had no illusions. If the couple ever faced a real threat, like the prospect of spending the rest of their days in an American or English prison, would they hold out and refuse to talk?

Highly unlikely.

The Khrenkovs had the power to destroy years of his pains-taking work. They were replaceable; the network wasn't. But Tolkachev would have to act fast, and harshly.

The second problem was what to do with the prisoner. Linge had told them all he knew, and was of no further use. They could liquidate him, which was simple enough, and make sure his body was never found, just to be on the safe side.

That was the approach Tolkachev was inclined to take, on the principle that a dead enemy is no longer dangerous.

But that was a decision he couldn't make alone. Russia and the United States had worked to create a façade of cordial relations. All sorts of fierce struggles were being waged behind it, but the façade had to be maintained.

Tolkachev took his fountain pen, wrote a memo a few lines long, and initialed it. Then he rang for an internal Kremlin courier. The memo was addressed to the only person with the power to make the decision.

For the first problem, the Khrenkovs, Tolkachev gave himself a couple of hours before taking action. He had the authority and the means to act on his own. He couldn't afford to fail, however. When he was younger, he'd hunted brown bears. A dangerous sport, because if you only wounded the animal, it often had the strength to kill you before dying.

Rem Tolkachev didn't want anyone touching his precious *lastochkas*.

The red light above his door came on; the courier was outside. Without a word, Tolkachev cracked the door open and handed him the note.

The CIA agent's fate was now no longer in his hands. The old spymaster would obey whatever orders he was given. But in his memo he had made his preference clear: liquidate an enemy who had already made a great deal of mischief.

CHAPTER
17

Nancy Cobbold was crossing the Thames on the Hammer-
smith Bridge, with its fretwork of green metal beams, when she
noticed an odd-looking bundle on the riverbank below. Something wrapped in a blanket lay near the grayish water lapping at
the sandy bench along the promenade.

It looked like a body.

Intrigued, she turned off Hammersmith Bridge Road and
stopped at a flower shop.

"I think there may be a body down on the Mall," she told the
florist. "I'm in a rush and don't have time to go look, but it might
be a good idea to call nine-nine-nine."

Having salved her conscience, Cobbold continued on her way
onto Great West Road.

Five minutes later, a police car appeared above the riverbank,
announcing its arrival with brief blasts of its siren. Two policemen
approached the body and carefully unwrapped the blanket. Inside
was a man wearing only underpants, bound hand and foot.

"They found him; he's alive!" shouted Richard Spicer. "They're
taking him to Hammersmith Hospital on Du Cane Road. I'm
heading over now."

"I'll join you there," said Gwyneth Robertson. "What shape is he in?"

"I don't know. I was on my way to the office when MI5 called."

Grabbing her attaché case, Gwyneth sprinted for the elevator, her heart pounding. After getting no news of Malko for three days, she had given up hope of ever seeing him alive again.

At the hospital, a pair of uniformed police officers were standing guard outside Room 422. Spicer flashed his diplomatic ID and went in. Two people were already present: a doctor in a white coat and Sir William Wolseley, the MI5 chief of staff.

"The medics say he's all right," said Wolseley. "He was drugged but doesn't appear to have been injured. They're going to run some scans."

"What has he said?"

"Nothing yet; he's barely awake. He almost died of hypothermia. He must've lain near the river for at least two hours, and it's been pretty chilly."

"Who dumped him there?"

"We don't know, but it must have happened before dawn. A driver spotted him an hour ago and alerted the police. He didn't have any papers, so it took a while to identify him."

"Was he tortured?"

"It doesn't look that way, but he has injection marks on his left arm."

At that moment, Gwyneth entered the room. She ran to the bed where Malko lay, his eyes closed. Aside from being quite pale, he seemed reasonably healthy.

"I think we should let Mr. Linge rest for a few hours," said the doctor. "I'll ring you as soon as he's in shape to talk."

When they moved out into the hallway, Spicer said:

"I think you can dismiss your two constables, Sir William. The kidnappers have released him, so he's in no further danger. I'm anxious for him to talk so we can find out what happened."

"I'm staying here," Gwyneth announced. "I've canceled all my meetings."

"Okay," said the station chief. "Let me know when he comes around."

As she finished getting dressed, Zhanna Khrenkov realized she hadn't felt this good in a long time. True, Alexei wasn't talking much—he was distant, and almost mute—but she figured the main thing was done. His attitude showed that he really had broken up with the bitch. Zhanna was counting on time for things to sort themselves out. She and Alexei had so much in common, he was sure to come back to her eventually.

She had decided to go to the Dorchester Spa in the morning, for once, because she had a lunch date at the Grill. She was meeting a concert organizer to arrange a benefit for the victims of the floods in Pakistan.

For his part, Alexei was going to his office in the City and wouldn't be home until late.

Zhanna dialed Petropavlovsk to ask Vladimir Krazovsky to fetch her Bentley from the garage, but the number rang for a long time without anyone answering. She tried twice more, then, in some annoyance, decided to take a taxi. She would phone from the Dorchester to have the security detail pick her up.

Mercifully, she only had to spend a few moments out on the Grosvenor Place sidewalk. Five minutes later, she was pushing the revolving door of the Dorchester and heading for the elevator.

An older woman seated on a bench in the lobby stood up and

fell into step behind her. They entered the elevator together. Absorbed in her thoughts, Zhanna didn't even look at her.

When the elevator reached the first basement level, Zhanna moved toward the door as it opened. So she didn't see the woman pull from her purse a small black automatic fitted with a long silencer.

Extending her arm, she brought the barrel close to Zhanna's neck and pulled the trigger twice.

Two muffled *pfut!* sounds were heard, very close together. The cartridges' powder charge was small, but their impact was enough to knock Zhanna out of the elevator and leave her sprawled under the spa sign with the silver lettering.

By then, the unknown woman had already pressed the button for the ground floor, and the elevator door closed. Moments later, she stepped out into the lobby. She left the hotel and crossed onto Deanery Street, where a dark-colored car was parked. Someone inside opened the door and she climbed in.

The car made its way to the A4 and headed for Heathrow. The woman opened the envelope lying on the seat next to her and took out the passport she would use to leave the country. Her flight for Rome was leaving in two hours.

A spa employee found the body a few minutes later. She rushed over, thinking Zhanna had slipped and fallen. It was only when she tried to help her up that she realized she was dead.

Very dead, in fact.

The staffer's screams brought other employees running. Within moments, the spa manager was on the phone to the police.

———

"Jesus Christ!" the CIA station chief shouted.

Wolseley had just told him that Zhanna Khrenkov had been shot in the Dorchester basement two hours after Malko's release.

"Things seem to be picking up," said Wolseley with classic understatement.

"I'm going over to see Malko," said Spicer. "Are there any suspects at the Dorchester?"

"Nobody saw a thing. It's as if Mrs. Khrenkov was killed by a ghost. The police found two .22 caliber shells in the elevator, but I doubt they will lead anywhere."

"Where's Alexei Khrenkov?"

"We don't know. Nobody's answering at the apartment."

"We need to protect him, immediately."

"I've already dispatched a team of watchers to his office," said Wolseley. "That's all we can do for now."

Spicer was already halfway to the elevator. His mind was racing as he tried to fit the pieces of the puzzle together: Malko's release, Zhanna's murder, and the events that preceded them. Suddenly he had a horrible thought, and quickly phoned Wolseley back.

"You better send a team to Lynn Marsh's office on Queen's Gate right away, Sir William. She may be in danger too."

Spicer knew how merciless the Russians could be. If they decided to eliminate a rung of their network, they would do a clean sweep. And Lynn Marsh was too close to Alexei not to be a target.

"He says he doesn't remember a thing!" said Gwyneth the moment Spicer entered the hospital room.

Malko himself seemed to be doing a lot better. He'd eaten a big breakfast and his color was good.

"Someone shot Zhanna Khrenkov at the Dorchester half an hour ago," Spicer announced. "Two bullets in the neck. No suspects. The killer must have used a silencer, because nobody heard a thing."

"Damn!" exclaimed Gwyneth. "They don't waste any time, do they?"

She paused, then said:

"Richard, since you're here, I'll go get some things for Malko from the Lanesborough. I'll be back in an hour."

When they were alone, the CIA station chief sat down next to Malko's bed.

"Do you really not remember anything?" he asked.

"Nothing at all," answered Malko. "I went to sleep in my bed at the hotel, and when I woke up, I was tied to another bed and blindfolded, in some place that I probably wouldn't recognize."

"Didn't you see anyone?"

"Yes, a man I think was a doctor. They took off my blindfold. He talked to me, but I don't remember what I said. And then I was in darkness again. They must have drugged me, because I don't remember being taken out of wherever I was."

"The hospital's running some blood tests. We'll find out what they gave you."

"It doesn't much matter," said Malko. "I'm beginning to understand what happened. We underestimated them. The Russians must have been watching the Khrenkovs and the people around them very closely. They immediately noticed me and my contacts with Zhanna and Lynn Marsh. They decided I was hostile, and took action."

"But why kidnap you?"

"They must have needed an explanation for what was happening. That's the only thing I can think of. They would never dream that Zhanna had contacted me first."

"They've got some fucking nerve!" growled Spicer. "I was very worried about you."

Their eyes met.

"I don't know why they didn't kill me," said Malko simply.

"We may never know," said Spicer. "The main thing is you're alive and well. In any case, we're sure of one thing: the network Zhanna talked about exists. And the Russians put a very high value on it."

"Where is Alexei?"

"Scotland Yard is looking for him."

"We have to find him. He now knows that the Russians want to liquidate him. They started with Zhanna, which makes sense, since she was the person responsible for the disaster. But I'd be surprised if they let Alexei live. The one thing we have to do is find him before they do."

Malko paused.

"My guess is there's a Russian kill team in London. As there was for Litvinenko. People who traveled here specially, whom we'll probably never identify. They may already have made the hit on Alexei, even if he didn't do anything wrong. If it hadn't been for Zhanna's insane jealousy, we would never have learned about the network."

"We have to break it up," said Spicer, "and the only person who can help us is Alexei."

"Who may already be dead," said Malko with a sigh. "But if he's still alive, I have an idea that might persuade him to cooperate."

"What's that?"

"Lynn Marsh."

CHAPTER

18

Glancing at the Cartier alarm clock on his night table, Alexei Khrenkov could hardly believe his eyes. It was ten minutes past noon! To relieve his obsessive brooding over the breakup with Lynn, he was taking sleeping pills, and they upset his normal sleep pattern.

The breakup hadn't been his choice, and he sometimes woke up dreaming that Lynn was lying next to him, that they were making love, or that he heard her silvery laughter.

He hurried to take a shower.

When he emerged from the bathroom, Khrenkov switched on his cell phone to warn his office that he would be late for his meeting. He was seeing a real estate agent who wanted to sell him an apartment building.

As he was closing his crocodile skin attaché case with the gold fittings, his phone rang. It didn't display a number, but he took the call anyway.

"Is this Mr. Alexei Khrenkov?" asked a man with a Cockney accent.

"Speaking."

"I'm Sergeant Burdett of Scotland Yard. Are you Zhanna Khrenkov's husband?"

"Yes, I am."

"There's a problem with your wife, sir. You should come to the Dorchester Hotel as quickly as possible. We can send a car, if you like."

Stunned, Khrenkov asked:

"What kind of problem? Can you put my wife on the line?"

There was a brief silence at the other end, then the policeman spoke again, sounding embarrassed.

"I'm afraid that won't be possible, sir."

"Why? Has she been arrested?"

"No, sir. She's been shot. She's in bad shape."

Khrenkov felt as if his legs had suddenly turned to stone. His head was spinning. Despite her morbid jealousy, Zhanna was the woman he'd always loved.

"Is it very serious?"

Sergeant Burdett cleared his throat and confessed.

"I'm afraid she's dead, sir. You better come right away."

Unconsciously, Khrenkov noticed the contradiction: if Zhanna was dead, then his presence wasn't urgently required.

"Very well," he said, "I'll be there soon. I'm not very far away."

Khrenkov put down the phone and stared at his reflection in the mirror. His brilliant mind had gone blank. He was trying to remember when he'd last spoken to Zhanna. Yesterday evening, maybe . . .

Then a wave of anxiety suddenly washed over him. He had the feeling he was caught in a black web, with an invisible hand gripping his chest.

If Zhanna had been killed, that meant he would be next.

The shock gave way to a kind of cold lucidity, as Khrenkov's mind started functioning again. He knew Russia too well to entertain even a glimmer of hope. The Kremlin had decided his fate, and the CIA agent's hovering around them had sealed it.

Like the Mafia, the Russians never left anything to chance.

Even if he hadn't done anything wrong vis-à-vis his handlers, he knew there was no appeal in a case like this. Once the sentence was pronounced, nothing could stop the *siloviki* from striking.

He, Alexei Khrenkov, was going to be killed.

For what felt like a long moment, he felt crushed. Then he roused himself and started planning his immediate future. He didn't want to die. Putting Zhanna out of his mind, he thought about what steps he could take next.

His accidentally sleeping so late probably saved his life, he realized. If he'd gone to his office at ten o'clock as usual, he would have been dispatched before his wife.

The thoughts were racing around in his mind. How would they kill him? They would try to catch him by surprise, of course. And who better to do that than the people assigned to protect him, the Petropavlovsk men?

Taking the bull by the horns, he phoned the head of the team. Krazovsky answered immediately.

"Hello, Vladimir," he said. "I overslept. You can send a car for me."

"They're ready for you, sir. They're waiting in your front hall."

Hanging up, Khrenkov took off his glasses and wiped them. So the killers had already arrived. Irina, the Moldovan maid, probably let them in. The fact that they came upstairs to the apartment meant that they planned to kill him there.

Khrenkov wasn't a violent man and didn't have any weapons in his apartment. But the two men waiting for him in the entry hall were sure to be armed. He put his glasses back on and went to his wall safe. First things first, he thought to himself. He took out several thick bundles of pound notes and dollar bills. Money was no problem, and he could get more in a number of places around the world.

Provided he could reach them.

He also took out his bright red Russian passport and stowed it in his attaché case with the money.

Without a very clear plan in mind, Khrenkov went to the front hall. The two men sitting on faux Louis XV armchairs stood up when they saw him. Khrenkov knew one of them—Grigory Lissenko, a regular member of the Petropavlovsk team—but not the other. He was of average height and well built, but smaller than him.

Khrenkov managed a smile, and in Russian said:

"Hi, there. I've never seen you before."

"That's right," said the man, meeting his eye. "I just arrived from Moscow three days ago. I'm at your service, Gospodin Khrenkov."

Khrenkov immediately knew that the man had come to kill him.

Lissenko opened the front door, and Khrenkov followed him out onto the landing, as tense as a violin string. He was sure they were going to shoot him in the elevator. The cabin was already there, and Lissenko pulled the grille aside to let Khrenkov in. The man from Moscow was still inside the apartment.

Keeping his voice steady, Khrenkov said:

"Just a sec, Grigory. I forgot something in my bedroom."

Moving as naturally as possible, he left Lissenko standing by the elevator and went back into the apartment.

After that, everything happened very fast.

Khrenkov kicked the front door shut, locking Lissenko out on the landing. Then he dropped his attaché case and rushed the Moscow man, wrapping his big hands around his throat. Feeling flesh under his fingers, he started squeezing with all his might. He shoved his victim violently against a console, knocking over a tall vase of flowers.

Once recovered from his surprise, the man fought back furiously. In silence, Khrenkov repeatedly slammed his head against the wall. He managed to knock the man off his feet and crashed down on him, kneeling on his chest while choking him. Gradually the man's eyes began to bulge from their sockets, and his blackish tongue lolled out of his mouth. He struggled weakly for another moment, then his arms slackened and he stopped moving.

Khrenkov released his grip only very slowly.

He looked at the Moscow man's face almost with curiosity. It was the first time he'd killed someone, and it gave him a strange feeling. Then he had a stab of fear. What if he'd been paranoid, he thought, and gotten carried away?

Khrenkov's heart, which was already pounding, sped up further as he searched the dead man and felt a pistol grip in an inside pocket. He pulled out the weapon, a compact automatic fitted with a long silencer.

So he hadn't been wrong.

Just to be sure, he slid the breech back, catching the coppery glint of a cartridge.

If he had followed Lissenko into the elevator, the Moscow man would have shot him in the back of the head.

By now, Khrenkov had forgotten Zhanna and Lynn; he was thinking only of himself. He dropped the pistol on the dead man's chest and stood up, listening hard. Their struggle had made a lot of racket. Irina was in the kitchen in the back of the large apartment, but Lissenko might have heard.

Khrenkov went to look out the peephole and was surprised to see that Lissenko was gone along with the elevator.

Grabbing his attaché case, he ran to the landing and buzzed the elevator. You couldn't park a car for more than a few moments on Grosvenor Place, so Lissenko would be forced to wait on Chester Street, which meant he wouldn't see Khrenkov when he came out.

His heart in his throat, he emerged from the building. There was no one in sight.

He ran to the curb and flagged a passing taxi.

"Saint Pancras station, and hurry."

Khrenkov looked at his watch. It would take twenty minutes to reach the Eurostar station. With a little luck he could catch a train for the Continent. At the train station, exit formalities were much more relaxed than at an airport. Besides, he wasn't a wanted man, at least not yet. His most ferocious enemies were still a few thousand miles away, in the Kremlin.

Absentmindedly, Khrenkov studied the traffic around him, counting the minutes. He was feeling a kind of dull anxiety, and it took him a few moments to realize why: he was thinking about Zhanna.

He would never see her again, never talk with her again. That hurt, the way an amputation might hurt. And he knew it would hurt for a long time—if he lived.

The taxi slowed down. They had reached St. Pancras. Khrenkov tossed the driver a twenty-pound note and dove into the crowd.

Richard Spicer and Malko Linge reached the Dorchester just as two nurses were loading Zhanna's body into a St. Mary's Hospital ambulance. A Special Branch sergeant greeted them.

"We're waiting for Mr. Khrenkov," he said. "He should be here soon."

"You spoke to him?" asked Malko in surprise.

"Certainly, sir. I think he was at home. I gave him the bad news with as much delicacy as I could."

Malko could feel the earth shifting beneath his feet.

"Did you tell him his wife had just been killed?"

"Yes, sir."

Malko gave Spicer a despairing look.

"We better get over to his place right away," he said. "We might still be in time. This gentleman can come with us."

Followed by the police car, they raced toward Grosvenor Place.

"We'll be very lucky if we find him alive," said Malko. "They're obviously wiping out the network."

When the two vehicles stopped at number 18, everything seemed calm. They went up to the top floor and rang on the only door. After a long silence they were considering leaving when they heard a woman's piercing scream from the other side.

The officer in the GK bulletproof vest who had accompanied them started pounding on the door.

"Open up! Police!"

On Track 11, the Eurostar for Brussels and Amsterdam gently pulled out of the station. Khrenkov watched the shabby buildings near the station pass as the train picked up speed, knowing he would never see England again. The immigration officer had barely glanced at his passport. In a few hours he would be far away, somewhere in Europe.

Khrenkov knew how to arrange his life in a material sense, but from now on he would be on the run around the world, a fugitive with the Kremlin's most deadly assassins on his trail.

Irina, the Moldovan maid, stood gaping in horror at the corpse in the entry hall, her hands on her mouth. The Scotland Yard sergeant was on his cell, calling his superiors.

"Khrenkov seems to have won the first round," remarked

Malko. The Kremlin assassin lay on the blue Chinese carpet, eyes bulging.

Picking it up by the barrel, an MI5 officer took the silenced pistol from the man's chest and carefully examined it.

"No manufacturer's marks," he said. "Made in-house, courtesy of our *siloviki* friends."

"Alexei Khrenkov was damned lucky," said Spicer.

Looking at the dead man's frozen face, Malko said:

"If we're going to have any chance of shutting down the network, we better find him before the others do."

CHAPTER
19

Even with all its sugar, Rem Tolkachev's tea tasted bit-ter. Two days had passed since he'd given the order to liquidate the Khrenkovs. Zhanna, whose fit of jealousy had caused the whole crisis, was dead, but her husband was nowhere to be found.

He had vanished after leaving the Grosvenor Place apartment, along with the *lastochkas* network operational workings, a secret that could be devastating for the Kremlin.

For the first time in his career, Tolkachev didn't know which tack to take. Should he try to lure Khrenkov home, or have him killed?

He hadn't done anything wrong, he knew. Thanks to Malko Linge's "confession," Tolkachev understood how the situation had developed. He had chosen to eliminate the Khrenkovs because the CIA was sure to keep the network leader under constant surveillance.

The swallows were leaderless, and the dead-letter boxes weren't being serviced.

Khrenkov must be wondering why the Kremlin had suddenly turned on him. He almost certainly didn't know about his wife's fit of madness.

Tolkachev gazed at the thick folder on his desk. It contained everything the Kremlin knew about Alexei Khrenkov: how the

former vice minister had worked his swindles, his various resi-
dences, and above all, where his main bank accounts were. Khrenkov would need that money eventually, Tolkachev reflected; that
might be a way to pick up his trail.

The man certainly wouldn't return to Britain, so that left New
York and Cologny, a Geneva suburb where Khrenkov owned a
luxurious villa.

The night before, Tolkachev had ordered discreet surveillance
of the brownstone and the villa. In both places, he had to tread
lightly, however. The Americans and the Swiss wouldn't take
kindly to this kind of foreign activity.

Fortunately, the situation wasn't urgent. For the time being,
Khrenkov had no reason to hand his network over to the Americans. He had plenty of money and might be hoping he could
escape the Kremlin's killers. Which gave Tolkachev time to decide
how to get rid of him.

The old spymaster reread the British newspaper clippings
describing the body found in the Russian millionaire's apartment.
The dead man had a gun equipped with a silencer, and the papers
naturally linked the killing to the shooting of the millionaire's
wife the same day, which also involved a silencer. The tabloids
portrayed the two events as a shoot-out between Russian oligarchs, noting that welcoming such people to Britain had its
drawbacks.

Having thought it over, Tolkachev decided he would first try
playing a wild card. He wrote a brief note to one of his people in
Cyprus. The instruction was simple: send Khrenkov a text asking
him to return to Russia to explain himself. Khrenkov had just
barely avoided being murdered, and the chances of his accepting
were minuscule, but it was worth a try.

If he came home, the problem was solved. If not, Tolkachev
would move to the next stage, which would require some plan-

ning. The members of the kill team he had sent to England had already left the country—except the one Khrenkov strangled, of course.

Tea and biscuits were arrayed on the maple table, as they were at all MI5 meetings. After pouring tea for his guests, Sir William Wolseley got down to business. Turning to Malko and Spicer, he said:

"We haven't been able to identify the man found in Alexei Khrenkov's flat. He had a false Cypriot passport and had taken a room in a small Kensington hotel."

"Hmm. That's not far from Dr. Marsh's office," remarked Malko. "I'm sure it's no coincidence. Maybe he'd been assigned to kill her as well."

"I'm afraid we will never know," said Wolseley with a sigh. "He will be buried under his false name, and I doubt he will be claimed."

The killer probably had a family, thought Malko. They would never know what happened to him, or where he was buried.

A spy without a name.

"What about Alexei Khrenkov?" he asked aloud.

"Vanished, I'm afraid. We have no evidence that he crossed any borders, but I doubt he's in the country. He probably left by train, paying for his ticket in cash and breezing through immigration."

"Is he on a wanted list?"

"No, he isn't. We're positive he strangled the Moscow killer, but right now he's only listed as a person of interest."

"So he could be anywhere. Do you know where he's likely to show up?"

"The FBI is watching his Eighty-Third Street house," said Spicer.

"I'd be surprised if he went to the States," said Malko. "He has enough money to start a new life with a new identity, and he'll steer clear of any risky business. If the Russians don't catch him, that is. They'll recruit a new person to run the swallows network, someone we know nothing about."

"And we'll be screwed," said the CIA station chief gloomily. "Just the idea that this guy knows all about that network makes me crazy."

"Unfortunately, Mr. Khrenkov has no reason to want to please you," said Wolseley with a hint of sarcasm.

A hush descended on the three men, gingerly.

The silence lasted for a moment.

"I have an idea that might get him to work with us," said Malko thoughtfully. He turned to the MI5 chief of staff.

"Tell me something, Sir William. Can Khrenkov be charged with murder, even if he might later claim self-defense?"

"I suppose so," said Wolseley with a frown. "Why?"

"It might be a way to slow him down, make it harder for him to travel."

"I can look into it. I'll take it up with a colleague at the Ministry of Justice, but he may take some persuading."

"What do you have in mind?" asked Spicer. "With money and good lawyers, Khrenkov can beat that kind of charge."

"That's true, but I also have a second idea."

Malko told them what it was, and they listened raptly.

When he finished, Spicer said:

"The plan has a lot of ifs, but I think it's worth trying."

"I'm also going to need your cooperation, Sir William," said Malko.

"You have it."

"In that case, wish me luck."

―――――

Khrenkov had the taxi drop him off across from the Cologny villa and rang the bell. He had deliberately not phoned ahead. His butler, Boris, a Moldovan he'd recruited in town, was in his shirtsleeves when he opened the front door.

"I didn't have time to warn you," said Khrenkov simply. "Incidentally, nobody must know that I'm here. If anyone calls, I'm traveling."

He hardly used the villa, which had been bought in the name of a Cayman Islands company. Few people even knew about it. Khrenkov paid Boris five thousand Swiss francs a month, and the butler would have swallowed his tongue if his boss asked him to.

"Make me some tea, please," said Khrenkov before disappearing into his office, whose bay windows looked out on Lake Geneva and the Alps.

Khrenkov had crossed Europe by train, and he was exhausted. He'd first taken the Eurostar to Amsterdam, then made connections to Dusseldorf and Basel. By staying within the twenty-six-country Schengen Area, he hadn't had to show his passport. Even the Swiss had dropped their land border controls, and people came and went freely.

As a result, nobody knew he was in Switzerland, the Russians least of all—though they could probably find out with a little effort.

Having finished his tea, Khrenkov opened the left-hand drawer of his desk, revealing a Sig automatic lying on a Hermès agenda. Under the somewhat flexible Swiss laws, individuals were allowed to own firearms. The pistol had been a gift from one of his bankers.

It was a life insurance policy.

But maybe a limited policy, because the Kremlin assassins had other ways of killing him.

Hefting the Sig, Khrenkov found its weight reassuring. He decided that he would carry it all the time from now on.

First thing in the morning, he would start building his new life.

He was about to fall asleep when his cell beeped: a text message, in Russian, origin not specified. It was a long text from one Vitaly Patashov saying that the oblast was prepared to reconsider the charges against him if he came to Moscow to explain himself. He would then be free to leave the country again.

Khrenkov couldn't help but smile. *Siloviki* never hesitated to use the most obvious ploys. Once in Russia, at best he would be shipped off to Siberia to play chess with Mikhail Khodorkovsky; at worst he would be immediately shot.

The Kremlin was clearly counting on the fact that he felt he hadn't done anything wrong. In a normal country, it would be in Khrenkov's interest to go home and work out a deal. But Russia wasn't a normal country. It was a totalitarian state where the Kremlin was all-powerful.

And the Kremlin was his enemy.

He switched off the light, leaving the Sig on his night table. The text message gave him some breathing room. It meant they probably wouldn't try to kill him right away.

Having checked with his colleagues, the Scotland Yard officer joined Malko in Richard Spicer's car. The other policemen were in an unmarked car parked on the Queen's Gate median, equipped with bulletproof vests and MP5 submachine guns.

"The young lady is still inside," said the officer.

Malko grinned at Spicer and said:

"Wish me luck!"

The CIA station chief watched as Malko went up to the door at 82 Queen's Gate. Lynn Marsh's dental office was on the second floor. He rang the bell, and a female voice came on the intercom:

"Doctors Marsh and Maple. Can I help you?"

"I have an appointment with Doctor Marsh."

He was promptly buzzed in. The two dentists shared a secretary, and she probably didn't keep track of all their appointments.

Upstairs, Malko found three people in the waiting room, so he took a seat and started reading an old issue of *Vogue*.

He was feeling tense. If he failed now, the Russian spy network would have a bright future ahead.

Twenty minutes later, a door opened to reveal Lynn Marsh wearing glasses and a nicely cut white lab coat. When she saw Malko, she froze.

"What are you doing here?" she asked in an icy tone.

"I came to see you."

"I don't have anything to say to you. Leave immediately."

She turned on her heel and walked back into her office. Malko followed and as she closed the door put his foot in the gap.

"I have to talk to you," he insisted. "It's for your own safety."

Glaring at him, she said loudly:

"Rose, call the police!"

"You don't have to," he said. "They're already downstairs."

Taking advantage of her surprise, Malko pushed his way into the office, closed the door, and turned to face her.

"And now, you're going to listen to me."

CHAPTER

20

Her lips pinched, Lynn Marsh was pale with rage. Taking her by the elbow, Malko led her to the window.

"Do you see the blue car down there on the median, with two men in it? Those are Special Branch officers. They're here to keep you from being killed. The way Zhanna Khrenkov was killed this morning."

Malko felt the tension abruptly go out of Lynn's body.

"What are you talking about?" she stammered. "Who killed her? Not Alexei, I hope."

"We don't know, but I'm pretty sure they were Russian secret agents. You shouldn't be surprised. Gwyneth Robertson must have already told you about this business."

"You know her?"

"Of course. I work for the CIA, in cooperation with MI5."

Lynn made a weary gesture.

"I don't want to hear about that stuff anymore."

"Don't you want to know why Alexei broke up with you? He was crazy about you."

A flash of interest lit up her eyes. He had touched a nerve.

"Why did he do it?"

"It's a little complicated to explain. I'll tell you over dinner."

After a moment's hesitation, Lynn took off her lab coat and

stepped into the next room. When she came out wearing a tailored white wool dress with black stockings, she looked quite beautiful again.

"Where are you taking me?"

"The Grill at the Dorchester; it's quiet. It's also where Zhanna was shot this morning, in the basement outside the spa. Two bullets in the neck. Is your car here?"

"Yes."

"Let's take it."

Lynn bid her secretary good-bye and followed Malko out. Her Mercedes was parked a little farther on. When Lynn started it up, Malko saw the Scotland Yard car fall in behind them and pointed that out to her. The young dentist made no comment.

She began to relax only when they were seated at a table in the back of the restaurant and she had ordered a gin and tonic.

"So tell me," she said. "Why did Alexei break it off?"

Malko talked for such a long time that Lynn's lobster bisque started to get cold. Anyway, she didn't seem to be hungry. She was drinking in Malko's words. He explained his theory, that Khrenkov had been forced to leave her so as not to attract the suspicions of his Kremlin masters.

Though it was quite cold by now, Lynn finally started eating the bisque.

Malko observed her.

"Now do you understand why you're in danger?"

"Not really."

"You don't know Russian intelligence," he said. "The people handling the Khrenkovs decided they were a security risk because of my presence in their entourage. Also, the fact that you and I met, twice. To them, I'm an enemy. So they decided to eliminate that echelon of the network, even if it hurts the organization. They shot Zhanna first, but Alexei somehow escaped being killed.

"He's on the run somewhere, but they're on his trail, and they won't give up. Remember Leon Trotsky? He was assassinated in Mexico twenty years after leaving the Soviet Union. An NKVD agent pretending to be an admirer put an ice axe through his skull. The regime in Russia has changed, but the methods are the same."

Looking very pale, Lynn put down her spoon.

"Do you think they'll kill him?"

The concern in her voice was palpable.

"If they can, certainly."

"My God!"

There were tears in her eyes. The woman was clearly still in love.

"You're one of the only people who can save his life," Malko said quietly, putting his hand on hers.

"Me, how?"

"We don't know where he is. We're guessing that he managed to get out of England."

"He has a house in New York and one in Geneva."

"Geneva, really?"

"Yes, but he almost never uses it. I don't even know where it is. He just mentioned it once."

"He probably won't go there," said Malko. "The Russians are after him, and they must know about that house. The only way to keep him alive is for us to find him before they do."

"What will you do then, arrest him?"

"No, we'll offer him a deal: his network in exchange for American protection. He'll be able to change his name and start a new life. He doesn't need money; he has plenty of that."

"Do you think he would agree?"

"I have no idea," Malko admitted. "But he knows they'll kill him, even if he didn't do anything wrong."

"So why do you need me?"

"Because we don't have any way to contact him. He obviously doesn't trust us, but he would trust you."

She stared at him balefully.

"So you want to use me for your dirty tricks!"

Malko smiled.

"No, this is a win-win situation. Alexei stays alive and we roll up a spy ring. But the plan entirely depends on you."

"On me?"

This was the moment of truth. Everything hung on the depth of Lynn Marsh's feelings for her lover.

Malko decided to make his pitch in stages.

"I think Alexei is still in love with you," he said. "He broke up with you so as not to put you in danger. Or because Moscow ordered him to. Either way, that's in the past. Do you still have his cell phone number?"

"Yes, of course. Why?"

"Because if you call him, I think he'll answer. Unless he's already dead."

After a long silence, Lynn asked:

"Why would I call him? I don't want to see him again. He's told me too many lies."

"Lynn, he didn't have any choice. And I don't think he ever lied about his feelings for you."

"And if I call him, what will I say?"

Malko's pulse sped up: the tide was turning his way.

"That you want to get back together. For better or for worse."

Malko now stopped talking and turned his attention to his lamb, which was delicious, to give her time to absorb his proposal. He watched her from the corner of his eye. She was clearly feeling overwhelmed, even finding it hard to eat. At last she put down her fork and looked at him.

"If I do this, what will happen?"

Malko was noncommittal.

"If my theory is right, you'll have a chance to restart your relationship," he said. Then he smiled. "Though it could cause some upheaval in your life."

"Why?"

"Yesterday, Alexei became a man hunted by Russian intelligence. He'll be hunted until his dying breath. He will never be able to live with you in London, for example. But that's another story. Will you call him?"

She slowly shook her head.

"I don't know. I have to think about it."

"Don't wait too long," he advised. "You're both in terrible danger."

Lynn suddenly paled again.

"I don't feel well," she said. "I want to go home."

"No problem."

Within minutes, he had paid the check and was escorting her outside. When the valet parker brought her Mercedes around, she turned to Malko.

"Would you mind driving? I don't feel up to it."

The Scotland Yard car was parked a few yards away, and when Malko took the wheel, it followed them. There wasn't much traffic heading west, as Lynn directed him across the Hammersmith Bridge and into Barnes, a neighborhood with a small-town feel. Finally they reached the Harrods Village development, a group of warehouses that had been turned into apartments.

It was a gated community with a guard at the entrance. Lynn's Mercedes had an electronic fob that automatically raised the gate, and she directed Malko to her underground parking space. Behind them, he could see the Scotland Yard officers talking with the guard.

Lynn didn't object when Malko followed her upstairs in the elevator. Her flat had high ceilings and was tastefully furnished with antiques. She switched on the lights, poured herself a large Chivas Regal that she downed in a gulp, and dropped into an armchair.

Everything was up in the air, and Malko was careful to respect her silence. It went on so long he thought she'd fallen asleep. When she spoke, her voice was hoarse.

"I've decided: I'll text him."

"Good. But he'll probably be on his guard. Mention something that only the two of you know about."

"He wanted to take me to the Seychelles a month ago."

"Didn't you go?"

"No, there was a problem with his passport. He has a Russian one that's only good for a few more weeks."

Malko managed to hide his reaction to this news. So Alexei Khrenkov had a weakness: he could no longer leave the Schengen Area. A serious handicap for a man on the run.

Holding her iPhone, Lynn typed a long message. When she finished, she looked up and said:

"Leave me alone now. I'm very tired."

Malko didn't insist. Outside, he saw the Scotland Yard car in a parking area. One of the policemen came toward him, his coat open on a bulletproof vest.

"From now on, don't let Miss Marsh out of your sight," said Malko. "She's in serious danger. I'll contact your superiors to confirm the order."

Seated at his desk in the Cologny villa, Alexei Khrenkov read and reread Lynn Marsh's text, wild with joy. It was all he could do not to answer her immediately, because he was in a very tough spot.

Before he could think of the future, he had to deal with his present, and above all, get a new passport. Ordinarily, the Russian consulate in Bern would renew his passport without any problem. Now, if he walked into the consulate, he would never come out again.

He had to find somebody, a forger maybe, who could fake the renewal stamps. But it wouldn't be easy. He closed his eyes, thinking of sunny Seychelles beaches.

The sight of the Sig lying on the desk brought him back to reality. A mountain stood between the present moment and the Seychelles. A mountain of difficulties, all of them major. Just the same, Alexei felt a fierce desire to live. Lynn still loved him. He put Zhanna out of his mind; he had to concentrate on his new life.

If he survived.

Almost without thinking, he began typing Lynn a text but was so rattled he had to start over several times. The message was very short:

I still love you. I'll explain everything. We'll be together soon.

Sending it left him feeling calmer, but a moment later, a blinding reality brought him up short: when he saw Lynn, he would have to explain a lot of things about himself. Living in London, she would have heard about Zhanna's death. He hoped that wouldn't be an issue between them.

Alexei went to check the doors and gaze at the lights of Geneva. Then he put the Sig in the night table and went to bed. He had trouble getting to sleep, aware that his desire to see his lover was even stronger than his fear of being killed.

The gray Mercedes 250 was parked at a bus stop on the Chemin du Nant-d'Argent. A Geneva bedroom community, Cologny was deserted in the evening. There were no pedestrians because downtown was too far away and the residents all drove. Also no cafés or restaurants. Just villas, each more luxurious than the last, with sweeping views of the lake.

So at this late hour, no one was likely to be curious about a parked car with two men inside, as still as statues. They were SVR agents and part of Russia's diplomatic delegation to the United Nations, but undercover. Fifty yards ahead of the Mercedes stood the gate to Alexei Khrenkov's villa.

The house looked empty. No light showed in any of the doors or windows. In fact, the men in the Mercedes didn't know if Khrenkov was inside. They were just a probe, part of the large-scale effort Moscow had launched to find his hiding place. There was no need to follow him. If he was in the villa, he would use his cell phone sooner or later.

And the trunk of the Mercedes held a device that could tap into a cell phone, provided it wasn't too far away.

The device, which had just arrived by diplomatic pouch, had been set to Khrenkov's numbers in the United States, England, and Switzerland. But it hadn't picked up any signals since the beginning of the two men's stakeout. They decided to quit at midnight and come back the next morning.

Suddenly a red indicator light on the control screen began to blink. The men exchanged a satisfied smile.

"Bingo!" whispered the driver.

The red light winked out. The call had ended. No matter; Alexei Khrenkov had been located, which was all that Moscow wanted. In addition, analyzing the intercept was sure to produce information about his plans.

"Let's go," said the passenger quietly.

He was anxious to find out whom Khrenkov had called, and what he had said.

CHAPTER
21

Richard Spicer was in high spirits.

"Congratulations, Malko!" cried the CIA station chief. "Thanks to you, we know that Alexei Khrenkov is stuck in Europe somewhere. He can't go back to Russia, and his expired passport keeps him from traveling freely. He should be receptive to our offer."

"Let's not get carried away, Richard. He hasn't answered Lynn Marsh's text message yet."

As soon as he woke up, Malko had raced to Grosvenor Square to report on his evening with Lynn Marsh. To say that Spicer had been enthusiastic was an understatement.

"MI5 has assigned an A4 team to protect her," said the station chief. "Around the clock, both at home and at her office."

"But they can't stop her patients from coming in," said Malko. "And if one of them is a Russian agent in disguise . . ."

Spicer mulled that over.

"You're right. I'll ask Sir William to station somebody in her waiting room. We'll let Marsh know. At the least sign of trouble, he'll step in."

"That could be too late," said Malko. "The Russians are dangerous and vicious, and my plan depends on Lynn Marsh and Alexei Khrenkov staying alive."

"We still don't know where he's hiding, do we?"

"No. I'm about to see Lynn for lunch; she might have news. Meanwhile, you could try to locate his house in Switzerland."

"He's not likely to go there, but we'll check. Anyway, the fact that he doesn't have a passport is a hell of a stroke of luck."

"For us, that is."

Rem Tolkachev savored his sweetened tea. He was feeling cheerful for the first time in days. The fishing had been good, on two counts. First, Khrenkov had been located. Second, the intercepted text message would help Tolkachev counter a CIA operation to spirit him away.

The spymaster found it hard to believe that Lynn Marsh had texted her lover on her own initiative. She'd been in contact with the CIA agent before; it had obviously been at his instigation.

Tolkachev had hatched a plan he felt should pay off handsomely. The trick was to first tighten the noose around Alexei Khrenkov, cutting off any possibility of escape. Then, when he was at bay, dangle the promise of immunity if he returned to Russia. He might be naïve enough to agree, knowing that he hadn't been at fault. That would be the most satisfactory solution. He could be interrogated to corroborate the revelations made by Malko Linge and give Tolkachev a fuller understanding of how events had played out. He could then be shipped off to Siberia or immediately executed, to protect state security.

Tolkachev would then have to find a new lord of the swallows. But once he did, he could reactivate the network.

His first task was to extinguish any hope Khrenkov might have of leading a new life. Which meant killing Lynn Marsh.

That would make waves, of course, because she was a British subject. But reasons of state trumped all other considerations in a situation like this. The diplomats could smooth any ruffled feathers later.

With his lover dead, Khrenkov would feel even more isolated and might be receptive to the Kremlin's overtures.

Lynn Marsh had dark circles under her eyes.

"I only have half an hour," she said to Malko when he entered her office. "Let's go to the pub next door."

He waited until they were served their fish and chips to ask the question that was on the tip of his tongue:

"Did Alexei answer?"

She nodded.

"Yes."

She took her iPhone from her purse and held it out for Malko to read Khrenkov's message. His pulse picked up.

"I was right," he said. "He is still in love with you."

"So it seems. But he doesn't tell me anything specific."

Women are never satisfied, Malko thought, smiling to himself.

"Lynn, he's a fugitive facing huge practical problems. Now we have to convince him to meet with you."

"Here in London?"

"Wherever he likes."

"What happens then?"

"You pass along our offer. Or I can come with you and present it."

Lynn turned pale.

"If I show up with you in tow, he's going to be furious."

"Okay, you're right," said Malko, quickly retreating. "Best you see him alone. I think it would be good if you sent him another text and asked for a meeting."

Malko was treading on eggshells, aware that the young

woman was torn between her love and the fear of being manipulated.

"I'll think about it," she said vaguely. "By the way, a plainclothes cop has been parked in my waiting room since this morning. Is that necessary?"

"Absolutely. When I said you were in danger, I wasn't joking. In fact, if any of your patients acts the slightest bit strangely, scream for help.

"We're dealing with cold-blooded, professional killers. The fact that you're a woman won't stop them. You can't trust anybody."

When they parted on the sidewalk, Malko reminded her:

"Don't forget to call Alexei!"

Alexei Khrenkov was depressed. It felt strange enough to be carrying a gun while walking the streets of a city as peaceful as Geneva, but he'd just suffered a major disappointment.

He'd been counting on help from a friend in the Russian U.N. delegation who had done him favors in the past. He took him to lunch at La Réserve, one of the best restaurants in town. But the moment Khrenkov mentioned getting a new passport, his friend shot the idea down.

"It can't be done, Alexei," he said. "Even if you offered some consular official a fortune, he wouldn't renew your passport. They have orders from Moscow."

Seeing Khrenkov's disappointment, he added:

"Why don't you come back and explain things? You know Russia: there isn't a problem that can't be fixed if you have enough money."

Driving back to Cologny, Khrenkov wondered if his friend wasn't right. But then a solution occurred to him that was both practical and pleasant. He was so eager to set it in motion that he pulled over well before reaching his villa and phoned Lynn. The call went directly to voice mail, which he'd expected. She never picked up when she was working.

He sent her a text saying that he absolutely had to see her before he made a trip back to Russia. Anywhere but London, he wrote.

Starting his car again, Khrenkov almost felt like singing. If he and Lynn could meet somewhere, he would give her the list of the network swallows for her to put in a safe place.

That way, if his Russian friends turned on him, he would have a bargaining chip. Khrenkov knew the workings of Russian power well enough to know that between forgiving a seven-hundred-million-dollar swindle and putting state security at risk, the Kremlin wouldn't hesitate.

Once again, Malko was bored stiff. He had nothing to do in London. The newspapers were no longer writing about Zhanna Khrenkov's murder. MI5 had skillfully leaked information about how the Khrenkovs had swindled the Moscow oblast. The British reporters swallowed this hook, line, and sinker, concluding that the oblast had sent a killer to settle scores with them.

Standard Russian procedure.

The day was ending, and Malko's phone hadn't rung once. Richard Spicer was busy with his many other obligations and didn't have much time for him. Thank God, there was always Gwyneth Robertson, who dropped by to distract Malko in every possible way whenever she could. As for Lynn Marsh, MI5 didn't need his help in protecting her.

Just as Malko was beginning to think that his plan wasn't

going to work after all, his beeping cell phone made him jump. His heart started to pound when he read the text:

He wants to see me somewhere in Europe. Lynn.

Things were moving again! Malko immediately called her office and asked the secretary to put Dr. Marsh on the line.

"I don't have much time," said Lynn. "What do you want?"

"I got your text message. What time do you quit work?"

"At seven thirty."

"I'll pick you up," he said, and hung up before she could argue.

"That's terrific," said Spicer, delighted to be pulled out of an interminable meeting. "As soon as you know where they're meeting, we'll arrange their protection, assign bodyguards."

"Don't get your hopes up yet," Malko replied. "It's already a miracle that we have a contact with Khrenkov. Lynn Marsh isn't about to let herself be manipulated."

"I thought you were able to seduce every woman you met."

"Not her," he said soberly.

Lynn eagerly drank the flute of Taittinger Brut that the waiter set before her. She was wearing her weekday uniform, the white wool suit and black stockings.

Malko had spent nearly an hour in her waiting room and begun to think she'd stood him up when she came out of her office, breathless and apologetic: the work on her last patient had been particularly difficult.

He discreetly signaled the waiter to refill her glass. The Library was very animated, and Lynn watched curiously as the female escorts came and went, each more beautiful than the last.

"Are they prostitutes?" she asked.

Malko smiled.

"Let's not cast the first stone. They're almost all Cold War refugees, and they haven't had an easy life."

Lynn turned her attention to a beautiful black woman in a clingy outfit that made the most of her assets. She was draped around a fat man with a mustache, who was letting his hand drift from her waist down toward the forbidden fruit.

"What about her?" she asked. "Did she come in from the cold too?"

"Life in Africa isn't easy, either," he said.

After Lynn had taken another sip of champagne, he asked:

"What did Alexei write, exactly?"

She pulled out her iPhone, swiped her finger across it, and held it out to him. When he saw Khrenkov's message, he practically whooped with joy.

"Did you answer him?"

"No."

"Really? Why not?"

"Because I don't plan to ever see him again."

Malko thought he had misheard, but Lynn Marsh's jaw was set, and she wouldn't look at him. For some unknown reason, his lovely plan had just collapsed.

Like a boxer staggered by a body blow, it took Malko a moment before he could go back on the offensive.

"I thought you were in love with him," he said. "He's apparently still crazy about you."

"That's true, but I've decided I can't go on like this," said Lynn, shaking her head slowly. "I've done a lot of thinking since getting his text. Your world scares me, and now Alexei scares me, too. If we get back together, I'll be frightened all the time. It's too much for me.

"You pressured me, and I shouldn't have agreed to contact him. I want a different life for myself. Just a quiet, ordinary existence until I meet somebody new."

"So you're not going to answer him?"

"I will, but I'm going to say I don't want to see him again. For my own good."

She finished the rest of her champagne.

"Please don't insist," she said, though Malko hadn't spoken.

Accepting her decision as gracefully as he could, he stood up and kissed her hand.

"I think you're making a mistake," he said. "You've gotten into this without realizing it, but you won't be able to get out so easily. You're in serious danger, otherwise Scotland Yard wouldn't be protecting you. And you're still a target for our Russian friends, even if you never see Alexei again."

She gave him a little wave, as if to dismiss his concern, and stood up to leave.

Next to them, the black woman's plunging neckline displayed three quarters of a bosom that proved that silicone had reached African shores.

Josefa Svoboda handed her passport to the Heathrow immigration officer sitting in his glass booth. She was so gorgeous, he had to make an effort to focus on the Czech document and its collection of British visa stamps. Josefa came to London regularly for fashion shoots. A slender six-foot model with cobalt blue eyes, she didn't go unnoticed. The officer watched as she joined the other travelers heading for the terminal exit. He would never get to sleep with a girl like that, he thought sadly.

Josefa gave the taxi driver the address of the Helen O'Brien Agency, the company that usually handled her bookings. She was in London for only forty-eight hours.

As he did every evening, the MI5 agent in charge of guarding Lynn Marsh picked up a photocopy of her appointments for the following day. This was a routine precaution, made easier by the dentist's cooperation. She highlighted her regular patients' names to avoid wasting time checking them.

The MI5 computers at Thames House scanned the new patients for links to a foreign intelligence service. Badly burned by Zhanna Khrenkov's murder, the British were taking the young dentist's protection very seriously.

———

Malko and Spicer were having breakfast in the CIA station chief's office. The mood was somber.

Malko had just related Lynn Marsh's decision not to renew her relationship with Khrenkov, concluding:

"Now we'll have to locate him ourselves."

Spicer raised his eyebrows.

"Oh, great! We don't know where he is, and even if we find him, he doesn't have any reason to cooperate with us anymore."

"There's still the problem with his passport," said Malko. "If he wants to escape the Kremlin's hoods, he has to be free to travel."

"That's not enough of a reason to betray the Russians," said Spicer. "If he gives us the swallows network, he can be damn sure they'll track him to his dying day. His wife is dead, and his girl-friend won't see him. He must be feeling pretty low."

"So what do we do?"

The station chief took a sip of the warm swill his office passed off as coffee.

"The only thing I can think of is getting Lynn Marsh to change her mind," he said. "If she won't contact Khrenkov, I can't ask MI5 to go on protecting her forever. They're putting a lot into this sur-veillance, you know—half a dozen A4 watchers."

Malko knew Spicer was right, and said nothing. Once the young dentist's connection with Khrenkov was broken, she would be less of a target for the Russians.

Maybe.

He was about to get up when the intercom buzzed.

"Sir William Wolseley on line two," the secretary announced.

Spicer took the call, and after listening for a moment, hung up and turned to Malko.

"We're going to Thames House; there's news. MI5 has spotted someone suspicious among the patients coming to see Dr. Marsh today."

"Josefa Svoboda is the daughter of Jan Sejna," said Wolseley. "He was the deputy head of the First Directorate in charge of StB foreign operations."

The StB was the Státní bezpečnost, Czechoslovakia's secret police under communism until it was dissolved in 1990, after the fall of the Berlin Wall. During the Cold War, the StB was overseen by Department 11 of the KGB First Directorate, in charge of espionage outside the Warsaw Pact countries.

"We spent a lot of time fighting the Czechs," Wolseley continued. "They were very active during the Cold War, and they did us a lot of damage. We know the Russian SRV and GRU have been contacting old StB veterans—reactivating them, in a way."

"What happened to Sejna?" asked Spicer.

"He died five years ago, in 1997."

"Do you think his daughter has any connection with the secret services?" asked Malko. "It says here that she's twenty-four, so she was only four when the Wall came down."

Wolseley sipped his tea before answering.

"That's true, and she often comes to London," he said. "She's a model and very beautiful. I don't think she's connected to an intelligence agency."

"So why did you alert us?" asked Spicer.

The Englishman smiled.

"While we were screening her, we thought we'd see why she was in London this time. And we discovered that she has a booker here, a certain Helen O'Brien, who runs a modeling agency."

"Is she Irish?"

"No," said Wolseley, shaking his head. "She was born Elvira Moscovici. She's a Romanian political refugee who came to England in 1985. She married an Irishman and later divorced him."

"Has she been up to anything suspicious?" asked Malko.

"Not as far as we know. Romanian defectors told us that Moscovici belonged to the Securitate, but since that was dissolved when Ceaușescu died, there didn't seem to be any further risk. We stopped our surveillance in 1990. This is the first time her name has appeared in a sensitive matter."

"Seems a little far-fetched, doesn't it?" asked Spicer skeptically.

Wolseley's left eyebrow shot up.

"You know the Russians always take the long view, Richard. You also know that they've tried to reconnect with the old Warsaw Pact agents. So finding two suspicious names among Lynn Marsh's patients demands a second look."

"You're quite right," said Malko. "What do you plan to do?"

"Take a few precautions," said Wolseley. "We don't want another Litvinenko affair."

Alexei Khrenkov stared at his cell phone, as if willing it to speak. It had been forty-eight hours since he texted Lynn Marsh. To allay his anxiety, he'd gone through every possible explanation, but the fact remained that she hadn't answered him.

And the more time passed, the greater his anxiety. Unable to stand it any longer, he banged out a new message, ending it with:

Darling, I love you, I need you, I want you.

A note of passion.

When his butler knocked on his office door, Alexei leaped to his feet, sending the Sig at his waistband crashing to the polished parquet floor. He kept forgetting he was carrying it. He picked up the gun and went to open the door.

"I fixed you a light lunch," said the butler. "A filet of sole and some fruit salad."

Khrenkov forced himself to smile.

"Thanks, Boris, but I'm not hungry. Later, maybe."

Until he got an answer from Lynn, he didn't feel able to eat a thing.

Standing at her dressing room mirror, Helen O'Brien adjusted the brooch on her jacket lapel and stepped back to see how it looked.

Studded with fake diamonds, the brooch had been bought at Harrods and then slightly modified. An almost invisible hole had been drilled in its center, to which a slender plastic tube was fitted. Its other end ran to a spray bulb like the one on a perfume bottle, hidden in O'Brien's right jacket pocket. Squeezing the bulb fired a spray of pulverized cyanide that would paralyze the victim's nervous system and kill within seconds.

An unknown Russian man had delivered the device to O'Brien two days earlier. He explained how it worked and gave her ten thousand pounds in hundred-pound notes.

That was just a down payment.

Since immigrating to Britain, O'Brien had been listed in the records of the Securitate, and later those of the SVR. Russian intelligence had contacted the most promising assets of the Romanian espionage establishment, to which she belonged.

A committed communist, she had never renounced her beliefs and was glad to be working for the Russians. Besides, without the SVR's discreet financial support, she would have closed up shop long ago. The modeling agency earned barely enough to pay the rent.

So when approached with a proposal by a stranger who knew the secret Securitate recognition code, she hadn't hesitated. It required one last favor, after which O'Brien would be brought to Moscow. There, the SVR would finance a modeling agency where she would manage the most beautiful women in Russia.

Added to the bank account that the SVR had regularly replenished since 1990, it made for a promising future.

O'Brien left her dressing room. To Josefa, who was waiting in the small room the agency used for casting, she said:

"Let's go!"

The young model eagerly stood up. O'Brien had suggested she get crowns on three of her teeth, and promised to cover the expense. They would see one of London's most popular young dentists, she said.

The two women went out into Fleet Street and hailed a taxi.

As usual, the waiting room was full. It served two dentists, and there were often a dozen patients there. John Bradwell, the resident MI5 agent, was reading the *Times*. He merely glanced at the two women who had just come in. He had memorized their faces and didn't need to study them to make what the Service called a "positive identification." He went back to reading the newspaper.

A half hour later, the secretary looked up and announced:

"Miss Svoboda."

The Czech model went into Lynn Marsh's office, closing the door behind her. The consultation took about twenty minutes, at which point Josefa appeared at the door and waved Helen O'Brien over.

"Come on in," she said. "Dr. Marsh can spare you a few minutes."

Josefa had explained that her booker needed a quick estimate for the treatment of some loose teeth.

O'Brien stood up, and Josefa took her seat. Bradwell watched as the women traded places, then crossed his legs and went back to the *Times*.

O'Brien sat down in the reclining chair as the dentist washed her hands and put a gauze mask over her nose and mouth.

"Open your mouth, please," she said.

O'Brien did so.

"Well, there's a lot of work to be done. If you're prepared to invest a couple of thousand pounds, I'll ask my secretary to write up an estimate."

"This one on the right especially bothers me," said O'Brien, pointing to a molar.

To see better, the dentist leaned closer, her face now just inches away.

O'Brien grasped the bulb hidden in her pocket and squeezed, firing a jet of cyanide out the hole in the brooch. It passed through the gauze mask and sprayed the dentist's nose and mouth. She staggered back, automatically ripping off her mask as she did. By the time O'Brien was out of the chair, she lay on the floor, unable to breathe.

Wasting no time, O'Brien calmly walked to the door and opened it. Then she turned around and said loudly:

"Thank you very much, Dr. Marsh."

Josefa was already on her feet, and the two women left the office.

Bradwell folded his newspaper. At last, he thought, he would be able to go to the loo.

For the next three or four minutes, nothing happened. Eventually, the secretary got curious as to why Dr. Marsh hadn't called the next patient and went to look through the office door.

From inside the bathroom, Bradwell heard a woman scream, and he rushed out, fumbling to zip himself up.

Reaching under his jacket for his gun, he raced out into the office. The dentist lay sprawled facedown on the floor in her white lab coat.

By the time John Bradwell came out onto Queen's Gate, the two women had disappeared. Pistol in hand, the MI5 agent ran to the Special Branch car parked on the median.

"Did you see two women come out?" he yelled.

"Sure," said his colleague. "They turned west onto Cromwell Road. Why?"

"They killed Inspector Hill!"

The officers in the car leaped out, and they all sprinted to Cromwell Road. The police car caught up with them there and drove as far as West Cromwell, but without seeing anything.

The women had vanished.

While one of the men called in an all-points bulletin with their descriptions, Bradwell returned to the dental office.

The patients had been evacuated, and a sheet draped over the body on the floor.

Lynn Marsh looked as pale as a ghost, and her features were drawn and haggard.

"What happened?" she asked shakily.

"We don't know exactly," said Bradwell, "but one of the women sprayed a deadly gas at Inspector Hill. She died instantly."

Lynn felt her legs failing her and had to lean on her desk so as not to collapse. When MI5 had suggested that a police officer who knew dentistry take her place to treat the two suspicious patients, she'd thought the idea ridiculous.

The woman, Inspector Jane Hill, wore an ultra-light bullet-proof vest under her white lab coat, but it hadn't been enough to protect her.

Brief blasts of a siren could be heard outside, and in minutes the office was invaded by policemen in uniform and plain clothes. Two burly officers came to stand on either side of the dentist.

"Dr. Marsh, you're coming with us. We're in charge of your protection."

She allowed the two men to lead her away. An unmarked police car was waiting downstairs, and they headed for Thames House.

Lynn wasn't able to think straight but would never forget the sight of the woman lying on her office floor, having died in her place.

She could hardly believe that people really wanted to kill her. Zhanna Khrenkov's death had seemed somewhat abstract. But here it was different, even if she hadn't faced the killer herself. Her hands clasped between her knees and her gaze vacant, Lynn wondered how she would get free of this nightmare.

The car stopped in front of a large black door that slid away to reveal a garage full of police cars. They had arrived at Thames House.

The officers escorted her to the small office of a woman who introduced herself as Inspector So-and-so—Lynn didn't catch her name. Someone brought them tea, and the policewoman set about trying to question the frightened young dentist.

"This is an extremely serious affair," she began. "We need to know absolutely everything that can help us."

Lynn nodded silently. The hot tea was doing her good.

But then she said, "I don't think I know anything."

Two floors higher, in the conference room next to William Wolseley's office, a half dozen men had gathered at the request of the MI5 chief of staff. Aides constantly brought in documents. A Special Branch representative sat glued to his cell phone, taking notes.

Looking grave, Sir William broke the silence.

"Our colleague Jane Hill was poisoned, apparently by gaseous cyanide. Death was practically instantaneous."

"Did you find the woman who killed her?" asked Richard Spicer.

"No, not yet. As with the Litvinenko affair, the operation was very carefully prepared."

"Anything going on at the *rezidentura*?" asked Spicer.

"Nothing," said Wolseley. "They were kept out of the picture. It's lucky we had our suspicions about Helen O'Brien. Otherwise Dr. Marsh would have been killed instead."

"What about the blond woman who was with her?" asked Malko.

"That's Josefa Svoboda. She was easy to locate, because she went back to her hotel. The Yard people are questioning her now. She doesn't seem to be part of the plot, and her story holds together. She says O'Brien suggested she have her teeth fixed and volunteered to pay for it. Naturally, she agreed."

"Why would O'Brien use her?"

"Because no one would think twice about a model wanting to improve her smile. Svoboda's in shock, afraid she'll never be able to come back to England."

"Couldn't she tell you anything about what O'Brien did?"

"No. It seems the women separated right after they came out. A car was waiting for O'Brien, and Svoboda took a taxi."

A heavy silence fell on the room.

For MI5 and the CIA, this was a major black eye.

Wolseley turned to Spicer.

"We're in an awkward situation, Richard. After what happened, we have to give Dr. Marsh total protection, but this isn't actually our case."

"I'm sure you understand the problem, Sir William," said Spicer. "The Russians are doing everything they can to protect the spy ring led by the Khrenkovs. They will only stop if one of two things happens: either they eliminate the people who can cause them problems—Lynn Marsh and Alexei Khrenkov—or we manage to shut down the network."

"Do you have an idea of how to do that?"

Malko chose to answer this.

"We might," he said. "Our plan all along was to convince Khrenkov to give us the network in exchange for our protection and the chance to live with Dr. Marsh—though not in London, of course. Only we had to convince him. Initially Dr. Marsh agreed to help, but then backed out."

"So where do you stand now?" asked the MI5 chief of staff.

"After what happened today, Dr. Marsh may well change her mind again. She didn't want to see Alexei Khrenkov again for fear of being sucked into a dangerous world. She now has proof that she's a target of the Russian services even if she doesn't see him. I'll try to persuade her to change her mind about breaking up with Khrenkov."

"She's here in the building right now," said Wolseley. "Why don't the two of you take her to dinner and see if you can convince her. If you can't, we'll have to take her out of circulation for a while and put her in a safe house."

Spicer and Malko exchanged a long look: this was their last chance.

The City Café was on John Islip Street, a short walk from Thames House. It was very British and quite empty, probably because it was still early and most MI5 staffers went home for dinner.

When Lynn Marsh entered the restaurant, she was moving like a sleepwalker: silent, eyes vacant, face drawn. Malko put a menu in front of her, but she didn't even look at it.

"I'm not hungry," she said faintly.

Spicer ordered roast pork loin. Malko opted for the lamb stew.

"I understand how shocked you must be feeling," Malko began. "We are, too. But your fate is in your own hands. Scotland Yard wants to put you in a safe house for a while, to protect you. Which doesn't solve anything in the long term."

Lynn gave them an anxious look.

"You mean I wouldn't be able to work?"

"I'm afraid not," said Spicer.

"That's impossible!" she blurted. "I'll lose all my patients!"

Malko gently put his hand on hers, and said:

"The other solution is to go back to the plan I first suggested: contact Alexei and persuade him to cooperate with us."

"I'll never be able to do that," she said quietly. "I'm scared. I just want to sleep for days and days. . . . Anyway, if I see Alexei again, they'll just keep after me."

"No, they won't," Malko assured her. "Once the network is shut down they won't waste their time seeking revenge. And you'll be able to live with Alexei if you still want to."

The waiter set a glass of water in front of her, and she eagerly drank it.

Malko leaned across the table, his face close to hers.

"Lynn, please text Alexei. Say you agree to meet him."

She didn't answer. She seemed to have lost the use of her vocal cords. When she finally spoke it was to ask, almost inaudibly:

"Where?"

Malko felt like jumping for joy.

"I'd suggest Vienna," he said. "Alexei can travel to Austria, even with an expired passport."

"Why Vienna?"

"Because we can protect you there."

In the back of his mind, Malko was thinking that Lynn Marsh would probably be safest at Liezen Castle. But one step at a time, he thought.

With exasperating slowness, Lynn reached into her purse and took out her iPhone. The two men held their breath while she typed a short text message. She showed it to Malko before sending it:

I will be happy to meet you. In Vienna. Lynn.

Once the message was sent, Spicer tore into his pork loin as if he hadn't eaten for a week.

"I hope you aren't making me do something stupid," she said with a sigh, gazing thoughtfully at her iPhone. "I want to go home now. And sleep."

Spicer snatched up his own phone.

"Let me see if I can arrange that."

In a way, William Wolseley was relieved to hear the news. Round-the-clock surveillance for Lynn Marsh was expensive and tricky. On the other hand, he wasn't quite happy about handing an Englishwoman over to the American cousins.

"And you guarantee you'll give her total protection?" he asked, sounding dubious.

"Absolutely!" said Spicer. "It's in our interest. And if Khrenkov says yes, as I think he will, we'll soon be leaving Britain with her."

"I'll need a sworn release from Dr. Marsh saying that she's going with you voluntarily and absolving us of responsibility."

"You'll have it, Sir William. As soon as we finish our dinner here I'll bring it to you personally. And we will take over Dr. Marsh's protection starting this evening."

Alexei Khrenkov immediately read the text message, and when he did, he read it three times. Vienna—well, why not? he thought. He didn't know why Lynn had chosen the Austrian capital, but it was a place he could travel to. His future still looked cloudy, but the thought of seeing her again gave him wings. He quickly typed a short answer:

Great! When and where?

Walking into the pantry, he asked Boris to make him a truffle omelet. Khrenkov was still carrying the Sig in his waistband, but his appetite had returned.

The two cars exited Thames House by the wide gate on Thorney Street. A CIA Mercedes led the way, followed by an MI5 escort vehicle.

Lynn Marsh had signed Wolseley's release. Actually, she would've signed almost anything to be allowed to go home. Two CIA case officers had joined the station chief and now sat on either side of her in the back of the Mercedes.

Khrenkov's answer arrived immediately, so all that remained was to arrange Lynn's flight to Austria.

Wedged between the two CIA men, she sat with her head back, dozing. They had to shake her awake when they reached Harrods Village, and it took her a few moments to find her keys.

Malko opened the door to the apartment for her, and she ran to her bedroom and collapsed on the bed, without even getting undressed.

Spicer looked at his watch and said:

"I'll have the cousins drive me back to the shop and leave my two guys with you. And this, too." He handed a 9 mm Glock to Malko, who slipped it in his belt.

"We're off to a good start," said Malko.

"I just hope she doesn't change her mind in the morning," said Spicer, sounding worried.

"I don't think she will."

"Of course there's one big problem," said the station chief. "When Khrenkov shows up in Vienna, he might be trailing a bunch of Russian thugs."

CHAPTER 24

Alexei Khrenkov ignored the view of the artesian jet ris-
ing above Lake Geneva, gleaming in the spring sunshine. Instead,
he was staring at the front page of the *International Herald Tri-
bune*. Someone had tried to kill Lynn!

He hadn't known about this when he answered the message
suggesting the meeting in Vienna, and was glad to realize she'd
texted him after the attack.

Khrenkov had made up his mind: he wasn't going to risk
returning to Russia. What had just happened in London proved
that the Kremlin had declared all-out war against him.

He folded the newspaper and began working out his travel
itinerary. It would be Geneva to Zurich to Bergenz, then across
Austria to Vienna. He didn't make reservations. He would buy his
ticket at the station.

But before that, there were some precautions to be taken.
Going to his wall safe, he took out a sheet of paper listing the
members of the *lastochkas* network. He sat down at his desk and
began to copy it, adding as many biographical details as he could,
including the cover names the swallows used in the United States.

Anna Kushchenko (Anna Chapman)
Mikhail Vasenkov (Juan Lazaro) and Vicky Peláez

Andrei Bezrukov (Donald Heathfield) and Yelena
      Vavilova (Tracey Foley)
Vladimir and Lidiya Guryev (Richard and Cynthia
      Murphy)
Mikhail Kutsik (Michael Zottoli) and Nataliya
      Pereverseva (Patricia Mills)
Mikhail Semenko
Pavel Kapusin (Christopher Metsos)

Then Khrenkov moved to a second document: the list of dead drops, electronic connections, and meeting places—mostly coffee shops and train or subway stations—where he hooked up with the swallows and paid them for their information.

Khrenkov smiled bitterly. The Americans would give a fortune for these documents. But he didn't need money. All he wanted was to live in peace with his lover, as far as possible from his former existence.

He stowed the precious documents in a large manila envelope. Now he just had to put it in a safe place.

"Boris," he called. "We're going into town."

The butler went to the garage and brought the Mercedes out.

Khrenkov went downstairs and joined him, with the Sig stuck in his belt.

"We're going to Crédit Suisse, on rue du Rhône."

The bank always rolled out the red carpet for Khrenkov, and no wonder: his account there held twenty-seven million dollars.

Heading down the villa driveway, Khrenkov peered around but didn't see anything suspicious. In half an hour, his life insurance would be in place.

———

Standing in the busy main terminal at Vienna International Airport, Malko scanned the arrivals screen. He was flanked by his old partners in arms, Chris Jones and Milton Brabeck, who had arrived from Washington the night before.

The husky CIA bodyguards wore their hair short and their trench coats long, hiding an arsenal worthy of a small aircraft carrier. Because the Vienna CIA station didn't have the manpower, they had been assigned to protect Khrenkov and Marsh against any unpleasantness.

Arriving two hours earlier, Malko had been greeted by his two favorite "knuckle-draggers" and his butler/bodyguard, Elko Krisantem.

The arrivals screen showed that a flight from Copenhagen had just landed. This was the flight Lynn Marsh had taken that morning, leaving London under a false name and escorted by Richard Spicer and Gwyneth Robertson.

Fifteen minutes later, the first travelers began to emerge. Malko stepped close to the two CIA men and muttered:

"If anything's going to happen, it'll be now."

Chris Jones didn't seem worried.

"If somebody so much as scratches his balls within ten yards of us, I'll waste him," he said. "Milt's ready too. If you knew what we're packing, you wouldn't have even bothered coming. Just show us the lady to protect, and we'll take care of the rest."

Milton Brabeck gave a low chuckle.

"Knowing the prince, I'll bet she's a hottie."

The two Americans only had to protect Dr. Marsh while she crossed the terminal. An armored Mercedes was waiting outside at the curb, along with an escort vehicle from the U.S. embassy.

More passengers now began to come out, and Malko held his breath. Then suddenly the tension eased when Gwyneth appeared, with dark glasses and a coat over her arm. She was followed by

Lynn, escorted by Spicer. The young dentist didn't seem to have completely recovered. When Malko went to greet her, she barely smiled.

"All's well," he assured her. "We'll be at the hotel in half an hour."

The two CIA men immediately took up positions around her, with Jones leading the way and Brabeck behind, walking backward. They practically shoved her into the heavily armored Mercedes, whose doors closed with a reassuring *thunk!* But Malko was still on edge. Vienna was a nest of spies, a place where the SVR and other Russian services were particularly well represented.

Lynn didn't open her mouth during the whole trip to Kaerntner Ring. At the Hotel Imperial front desk, she only had to scrawl a vague signature before Malko and Gwyneth led her up to her suite. The two guards took up positions in the hallway.

"You can take a bath if you like," Gwyneth said to her. "You're completely safe here. I'll be with you all the time, and Malko is in the next suite."

Lynn took off her jacket and lit a cigarette.

"Do you know where Alexei is?" she asked.

"No, I don't," Malko admitted. "But he knows where you are, so he should be here soon."

That was an example of the power of positive thinking, disregarding the likelihood that Khrenkov would show up with a slew of spooks on his heels.

Malko went down to the lobby and settled in to wait. He was the only one of them who could recognize Khrenkov. And the Russian didn't know where Lynn Marsh was, or what name she was registered under.

The train from Innsbruck slowly pulled into Vienna's main train station.

Khrenkov was in the lead car. He'd spent the trip studying his fellow passengers, without spotting any suspicious faces. The Sig was in his raincoat pocket with a round in the chamber. To his key chain, Khrenkov had added the key to the Crédit Suisse safety-deposit box. He also needed a code that gave access to the vault. The Kremlin would expect something sophisticated, so Khrenkov had simply chosen his birth date.

His plan was simple. Once in Vienna he would arrange a meeting with an SVR representative in a public place and offer him a deal: if the Kremlin left him alone to live in peace with Lynn Marsh, the *lastochkas* information would stay in the Crédit Suisse vault forever. Khrenkov was no intelligence agent. All he wanted was to enjoy his money and his mistress.

Hailing a taxi, he gave the Hotel Imperial's address. On this, his first visit to Vienna, Khrenkov was impressed by the majesty of the Austro-Hungarian Empire–era buildings.

When he'd left the Cologny villa that morning, he'd taken a basic precaution, telling Boris that he wanted to leave the house without being seen. So he went to the garage and climbed into the Mercedes's enormous trunk. The Moldovan respectfully closed the lid on him and drove out of the garage. Nobody watching the house could tell that the car had a passenger. Boris drove to the second subbasement in the vast Rhône parking garage, where he let his boss out. Khrenkov exited onto Quai du Général Guisan and took a taxi to the airport.

"We're at the Hotel Imperial, *mein Herr*," the cabdriver announced.

They had just pulled up at 16 Kaerntner Ring.

Khrenkov paid and entered the hotel lobby, which looked vast enough for Versailles. He felt anxious. How would he find Lynn?

He didn't have long to wonder. As he headed for the front desk he spotted a familiar face: Prince Malko Linge, the man at the root of all his troubles!

Khrenkov stopped dead, about to turn and leave.

But the CIA operative was already walking toward him, a friendly smile on his face.

"This isn't a trap, Gospodin Khrenkov," Malko said in Russian. "I'm only here to help you. Without our involvement you would have never seen Lynn Marsh again. We're the people who thwarted the attempt to kill her."

"Where is she?" Khrenkov croaked.

"She's here in the hotel," he said. "But before you see her, I'd like to have a talk with you."

Rem Tolkachev had summoned General Pyotr Ribkin to report on developments in the Khrenkov operation. Though a respected senior military man, he stood shifting from foot to foot in the spymaster's little office.

"Alexei Khrenkov has just reached Vienna, Gospodin Tolkachev," he said. "We have been following him from Geneva since intercepting his cell phone communications."

"What about the Marsh woman?"

"She has disappeared from her home and office in London and is not taking any new appointments."

"She's almost certainly in Vienna too," said Tolkachev.

After the botched killing at the dental office, Helen O'Brien had made her way to Russia by way of Moldova and Transnistria. The spymaster didn't blame her. No one had thought to give her a photograph of Lynn Marsh.

In a way, Tolkachev was glad O'Brien was out of England. With MI5 and Scotland Yard up in arms, a second attempt on Marsh would be suicidal.

It would be much easier in Vienna.

"What are your orders, Gospodin Tolkachev?" asked the general nervously.

"First, locate the two targets. When you do that, you'll be given your instructions."

After Ribkin left, Tolkachev lit a cigarette. He was facing a delicate dilemma: Could the swallows network still be saved? As far as he knew, none of its members had yet been identified. Zhanna Khrenkov hadn't had time to do any damage, and Lynn Marsh didn't know anything. Which left Alexei Khrenkov.

A ticking time bomb.

Looking weary behind his steel-rimmed glasses, Khrenkov listened to Malko impassively. It was the first time the two men had had a real conversation.

Malko laid out the American proposal: Khrenkov and Marsh would be taken to the United States, given passports and new identities, and protected for a long time. This was something the CIA and the FBI knew how to do.

"So you and Dr. Marsh will be able to live wherever you like," he concluded.

Khrenkov eventually broke the silence that followed.

"I need to talk to Lynn. Where is she?"

"I'll take you up to her."

The Russian followed him without a word. When Malko knocked on the suite door, Gwyneth opened it, then immediately stepped aside. Malko glimpsed Lynn in an armchair in the living room.

He discreetly waved Gwyneth out of the suite, and they went downstairs together.

The final act had begun.

For a moment, Alexei Khrenkov and Lynn Marsh just gazed at each other, almost shyly.

Then he rushed to her. Their bodies collided and remained welded together. His face buried in her hair, Khrenkov muttered something in Russian that she didn't understand. At last she lifted her face to him, and they shared a passionate kiss.

They stood in each other's arms, breathlessly swaying on the flowered carpet, unable to let go. It was the first time they'd touched since the Royal Garden Hotel in London.

Khrenkov led the young woman to a yellow sofa with big cushions, and they tumbled onto it together. He started taking off her clothes roughly and clumsily. He unbuttoned her blouse, then pulled down her bra and pressed his face to her lovely breasts.

Lynn strained excitedly against her narrow skirt to spread her legs, eager to receive him. She shuddered as he took one of her nipples in his mouth. Moaning with desire, she took Khrenkov's head in both hands and pulled it even closer.

He dropped to his knees on the carpet. Releasing Lynn's breast, he shoved his face between her thighs. She bucked like a wild horse, and a seam on her skirt split, baring her thigh to the crotch. Now out of control, Khrenkov yanked at the black nylon triangle of her panties, ripping them.

Lynn lay back on the sofa, one leg draped over an armrest, and gave a hoarse cry when her lover roughly entered her. He started violently thrusting.

They were both too excited for it to last long. With a final thrust, Khrenkov pushed deep into her and came with a shout.

After a moment, he pulled out partway. He had lost his glasses in the melee, and his vision was blurry.

"*Ya lubliou tebya*," he murmured—I love you.

Lynn hugged him tight, still feeling his stiff cock inside her. In just a few minutes he had erased weeks of terror.

She would never leave him again.

General Ribkin had returned to Tolkachev's office with the latest information. In Vienna, his men had seen Alexei Khrenkov entering the Hotel Imperial. They also saw that the hotel was crawling with people who could only be CIA.

That was a bad sign, thought Tolkachev. The presence of the Americans meant Khrenkov was betraying the *lastochkas*. And in that case, there was nothing left for the Russians to do.

Except to make an example of him.

The spymaster looked up at Ribkin.

"Liquidate both of them," he said quietly, "with as little collateral damage as possible."

The general's face betrayed nothing. This wasn't the first time he'd been given an impossible assignment. The Americans were professionals, and they would be on their guard, so he was sure to lose some men. He hated that, but you didn't disobey an order from the Kremlin.

The spymaster already seemed to have turned his mind to other things. He stood and genially walked the general to the door.

It had been four hours since Malko brought Khrenkov up to the hotel suite. Richard Spicer and Gwyneth Robertson were waiting out in the hallway. Chris Jones and Milton Brabeck were stationed in the lobby. Though at loose ends, the two guards were on high alert. Malko had warned them that they were up against a determined team of the best Russian intelligence agents.

Malko glanced at his watch.

"I'm going upstairs," he said.

Gwyneth was inside Suite 522, and Spicer on a bench opposite the elevator. Malko rang the suite doorbell once, twice, three times without result. Finally, he leaned on it until Lynn Marsh finally opened the door. She was wearing a terry-cloth robe and no makeup. She looked annoyed.

"What do you want?"

"I need to talk to you and Alexei. The less time you spend in Vienna, the better. The Russians are going to do everything they can to kill you."

Over her shoulder, Malko glimpsed Khrenkov coming out of the bedroom, also wearing a bathrobe. The young woman stepped aside to let Malko in, and the three of them sat down around a coffee table. The two lovers were glowing. They barely reacted when Malko asked:

"What have you decided? We can't stay here forever. Are you going to cooperate with us?"

The Russian took off his glasses and toyed with them.

"I don't know yet," he admitted. "I'd rather not betray them. They would never forgive me."

"They already want to kill you, Alexei. Like they did Zhanna."

As if he hadn't heard, Khrenkov went on calmly:

"I phoned somebody at the embassy. I'm meeting him later."

Malko felt his blood run cold.

"Where, at the embassy?" If that were the case, Khrenkov would never come out alive.

"No, at a café."

He took a piece of paper from his pocket and read from it: "Café Central, on Herrengasse."

A classic Viennese gathering place, Café Central featured art nouveau wood paneling, Gothic vaulted ceilings, white chandeliers, and big marble columns. All Vienna went there for the white chocolate cake and Einspänner—strong coffee with a dollop of whipped cream. While in exile in Vienna during World War I, Leon Trotsky was a regular customer.

"Why are you meeting them?" asked Malko.

"I'm going to offer them a deal. I've put the list of my network agents in a safety-deposit box in Switzerland. If the Kremlin leaves me alone, the list will stay there forever. But in case of my death, the bank has orders to give the list to the American embassy in Bern."

Malko was dumbfounded.

"The Russians will never agree to that! To them, you're too much of a threat."

Khrenkov shook his head.

"I want to try it, anyway," he said stubbornly.

"And you two have talked this over?"

"Of course. And Lynn agrees."

Malko could sense that he wouldn't be able to change Khrenkov's mind.

"What time is your meeting?"

"Five o'clock."

"All right. We'll arrange protection for you at the café."

———

The main room at Café Central was crowded, as usual. Customers sat at little tables or on long benches along the walls. Light filtered through high, arched windows. A grand piano stood in the middle of the room. The café seemed not to have changed in a century, though in fact it had recently been remodeled.

There were few women; they still preferred tea rooms, even after smoking in the café was banned. Most of the customers who came alone ordered coffee and spent their time perusing the newspapers clipped to wooden rods.

Malko looked around without spotting Khrenkov, though he knew he had entered the café. When he went into the next room, he saw him at a table facing a man in an ill-fitting suit with the square, inexpressive face of an apparatchik.

Malko went back out to Herrengasse, where the CIA guards were waiting in an embassy car.

"Our customer is in the second room," he explained. "It's empty, so pick a table where you can watch the entrance and make sure nobody else comes in."

The two Americans got out of the car with a clinking of weaponry. Chris Jones was carrying what looked like a black attaché case. In actuality, it unfolded into a bulletproof shield that could stop a .357 Magnum slug.

The second car remained at the curb, in radio contact with him.

Malko went back into the restaurant and took a table near the piano, from which he could see the two Russians.

Vladimir Robov was listed as a second secretary at the Russian embassy, and his soft voice and elegant language made him quite convincing in his role as a diplomat. In fact, he was a colonel in the GRU, the military intelligence service.

"I quite understand your anxiety," he told Khrenkov soothingly, "but Rem Tolkachev would like you to come to Moscow to explain what happened. I know that you're not to blame for any of this, but were dragged into it by your wife's jealousy."

"You killed her!" said Khrenkov sadly.

"We have to defend the *rodina*," said Robov, unmoved. "Zhanna made a very serious error. You didn't." He paused. "So, what should I say to my superiors?"

"Tell them I'll think it over," said Khrenkov.

"You're wrong not to trust me," said Robov. "In fact, I'm prepared to prove our sincerity in resolving this. Do you have your passport on you?"

"Yes, I do."

"It expires in twelve days, I believe. Give it to me, and we'll renew it for five years, without any restrictions. I hope that will make it clear where your interest lies. The Americans want to use you, not help you. We would like to work things out in a way that satisfies everyone. I have always favored negotiated solutions."

Coming from Robov, that was a sick joke. During the 1989 Tbilisi riots, the GRU colonel had picked up a shovel and cheerfully beaten anti-Soviet demonstrators to death.

Khrenkov hesitated. An expired passport wasn't worth much, he knew. He handed it over.

"I'll have it brought to you at the Imperial tomorrow," said Robov, pocketing it. "Shall we meet the next day, at the same time? You can give me your final answer then. If it's yes, I'll accompany you back to Moscow myself."

Robov put a ten-euro note on the table and headed for the door. Khrenkov watched the massive figure disappear. He felt torn, but something about the man from the embassy inspired trust. Then he remembered something and caught up with him as he was leaving the café.

"Gospodin Robov," he called. "If I accept your proposal, can my friend Lynn Marsh accompany me to Moscow?"

Stunned by so much naïveté, it took Robov a moment to produce a warm smile.

"Absolutely! I will give her a tour of our beautiful capital myself."

"You're out of your mind!" Lynn screamed. "You want to go to Russia after those people tried to kill me? Never!"

Khrenkov cowered under the barrage of reproaches. The dentist, who'd been getting ready for a romantic evening, was furious. He didn't know which way to turn and eventually took her in his arms.

"Please don't be angry!" he said. "You know I would never do anything without you."

Lynn relaxed a little and lit a cigarette. She felt caught between two worlds, aware that her past life was over. More calmly, she said:

"I'm going to be sacrificing many things for you: my life in London, my friends, my job. And I know that from now on I'm going to be living in fear. But too bad; I love you."

"What do you want to do?"

"You're the one who's going to do it: take the American offer. I want to go far away, somewhere sunny. I want us to enjoy life."

"All right," he said. "I'll tell them I'll do the deal."

Malko hadn't spoken with Khrenkov since the Café Central meeting. When he saw the Russian emerge from the elevator and walk toward him, he crossed his fingers, silently hoping that he hadn't been taken in.

"We have to talk," said Khrenkov.

They went into the empty tea room, and the two CIA men immediately went to stand guard at the entrance.

"I've decided to accept your offer," he said.

The tension in the pit of Malko's stomach abruptly eased.

"I think that's the right decision," he said soberly. "After that, you won't be in any further danger."

"I want to leave Europe, with Lynn. As soon as possible."

"That will take a little time to arrange," said Malko. "The Russians have to completely lose your trail, and that means false papers and a secret departure. We'll need a couple of days."

"I don't need any papers for the time being," said Khrenkov. "When I get my Russian passport back, it will be extended for five years."

To a dubious Malko, Khrenkov outlined Robov's apparently generous offer.

"That seems dangerous. Are you sure you can trust Robov? The man you met is no diplomat," said Malko, who had been briefed by the Vienna CIA station chief. "He's a GRU colonel with a reputation for viciousness. I doubt he'll give you a passport without wanting something in return."

"He's doing it to encourage me to go to Moscow to explain myself."

"That's crazy! You'd never come back, Alexei!"

"I know that. I wouldn't feel safe on Russian soil. But here, it's another story. And I can buy myself all the protection I need."

After a pause, Malko continued.

"Incidentally, when are you going to give us your network list?"

"I don't have it here. As I said, it's in a safety-deposit box in Geneva."

"So we'll have to travel through Geneva. After that, your worries will be over."

Malko smiled at him.

"Since that's all settled, I'd like to invite you to dinner at a place I know. My friend Alexandra will join us, and we'll be protected."

"Good. I'll go tell Lynn."

The Drei Husaren was another Vienna institution. Founded by three hussar officers of the Austro-Hungarian Empire, it featured hearty, traditional Austrian cuisine. With its mirrors and woodwork, the VIP dining room to the right of the entrance was reminiscent of Maxim's.

"Hasn't your friend arrived?" asked Khrenkov.

"She'll be here any minute," said Malko with a slightly forced smile. Alexandra ought to be on her way, driving from Liezen Castle.

He glanced over at Lynn Marsh. The young dentist looked radiant and relaxed. She was wearing the same scarlet dress as at Christie's, and Malko found himself staring at her bosom.

Khrenkov was holding her hand as if afraid someone would steal her.

Suddenly Malko saw Alexandra framed in the doorway. Her heavily made-up mouth looked enormous, and her décolletage was so deep it made Lynn's outfit look like a first communion dress. Alexandra's gaze fell on the young woman with the affectionate interest a cat might show for a mouse. If her green eyes had been lasers, Lynn Marsh would have been vaporized.

Malko made the introductions, and Alexandra sat down next to him. He familiarly put his hand on her thigh and felt the curve of a garter belt. She was wearing her combat uniform.

And was more desirable than ever.

While the other couple studied the menu, he slowly slid her dress up her long legs and whispered:

"I'm eager to get back to the Imperial."

"Do you really feel like having sex?" she asked, almost without moving her lips. "Didn't she satisfy you?"

Unaware of this incendiary dialogue, Lynn was struggling to decipher the German on the menu. The meal passed fairly quickly: they had truffle soup followed by *Tafelspitz*, a boiled beef dish that was the specialty of the house.

From time to time Malko looked over to check on Jones and Brabeck in the other room. They were peering at their *Tafelspitz* with deep suspicion.

Malko ordered a bottle of champagne to go with dessert, and the party toasted the future.

They took two armor-plated American embassy cars to return to the hotel.

On the way, Alexandra turned to him and asked coolly:

"Did you fuck her a lot?"

"Of course not!" he protested. "Alexei is crazy about her."

"But what about her?" she asked sarcastically. "She likes sex. You can see it in her eyes."

Malko chose not to pursue this high-risk conversation. Instead, as soon as they reached their hotel suite, he took Alexandra in his arms and stroked her dreamy ass. He slid down the zipper of her skirt, and it fell to the carpet, revealing long, black-clad legs and a white garter belt.

"Do you really want to fuck me?" she asked.

Before Malko could answer, a woman's cry came through the wall to the suite next door. Alexandra's lovely lips curled back in an appreciative smile.

"I think your friend Alexei is doing a Cossack number on her."

Suddenly Malko imagined Khrenkov fucking Lynn Marsh and immediately got a hard-on. Alexandra noticed it when he unzipped his pants.

"I want you," he said, starting to caress her.

"Are you sure it's really me you want?"

Alexandra's eyes were a bit glassy, and when he fingered her, he discovered that Lynn Marsh's shout had moved her as well. He took her by the hips and turned her around, pushing her over to the bed. Instinctively she arched her back. He spread her thighs with the seamed stockings and plunged in all at once.

It was wonderful to be with her again.

A second shout came through the wall, hoarser than the first, and Malko felt his heart start to pound. He pulled out of Alexandra, set his stiff cock a little higher, and thrust hard, drawing from Alexandra a cry as piercing as Lynn's.

The sexual marathon next door must have continued all night, because Alexei and Lynn didn't show up for breakfast, just had some food sent to their room.

It was about three in the afternoon when a small man came through the Imperial's revolving door. A skinny figure with a sunken chest, he looked like a sick ferret.

Automatically sizing him up, Jones and Brabeck decided he wasn't a threat. Besides, the hotel lobby was so open it would be ludicrous to try anything there.

"I'm from the Russian embassy," he told the front desk. "I have a document for Herr Alexei Khrenkov."

"I'll make sure he gets it," said the clerk.

"No, I have to deliver it personally," said the unknown man, without raising his voice.

The clerk phoned Khrenkov's suite and relayed the message.

"He'll be right down," he said.

Malko was in the hotel shopping gallery when his cell phone vibrated.

"They brought my passport," Khrenkov announced triumphantly. "They kept their word."

Malko immediately went down to the lobby and marched over to Jones and Brabeck. They were sprawled in big armchairs and looked bored.

"Did somebody come in just now?"

"Yeah," said Jones. "The skinny dude over by the front desk."

"He's Russian, and he's bringing Mr. Khrenkov his passport. Search him."

"No sweat," said Brabeck.

The two men jumped up and went to stand on either side of the man, whose head barely reached their chests.

"We're with the hotel security, sir," said Jones in English. "We'd like to pat you down."

Without waiting for an answer, Brabeck ran his hands carefully all over the man and didn't find anything heavy or sharp in his pockets or anywhere else.

"Thank you, sir," said Jones.

The two men went back to their armchairs. As Jones walked by Malko, he said:

"He's clean."

Just then Khrenkov emerged from the elevator and headed for the front desk. Malko watched as he exchanged a few words with the messenger from the Russian embassy. The man took out a clear plastic envelope from an inside pocket and handed it to Khrenkov, then walked toward the revolving door.

Alarmed, Malko noticed that he was wearing gloves, even though the weather was warm.

Looking delighted, Khrenkov slit the plastic envelope, pulled out a passport with a bright red cover, and opened it.

About fifteen seconds, and then he suddenly turned pale, opened his mouth as if unable to breathe, and began to stagger. Malko was already rushing over but had no time to reach him. Dropping the red passport, Khrenkov collapsed on the flowered lobby carpet.

Seeing Alexei Khrenkov slump to the floor, Jones and Brabeck leaped from their chairs. The messenger from the Russian embassy had gone out the hotel's revolving door.

"Get that man!" Malko yelled as he hurried over to Khrenkov.

The two CIA guards ran out to the Kaerntner Ring to see the thin man striding quickly toward Wiedner Hauptstrasse.

They pelted after him, shoving passersby aside, and were within a few yards when he turned and looked around. Seeing the two men, he ran to a black Mercedes stopped by the curb with a driver at the wheel.

"Freeze!" yelled Jones.

The man either didn't understand English or didn't feel like stopping. He jerked the Mercedes door open and was about to jump in when they opened fire, Jones with a .357 Magnum Colt and Brabeck a twelve-round Glock. As he clung to the car door handle, the bullets' impacts tossed him around like a rag doll.

Terrified by the fusillade, pedestrians dove for cover under the arcades.

The Mercedes driver hit the gas with the car door still open, ran a red light at the intersection, and turned hard into the Opernring, narrowly missing a tram.

The two Americans examined the skinny man now sprawled

on the sidewalk. He'd been hit a dozen times and was quite dead. As the passersby slowly began to emerge from shelter, the Americans holstered their guns.

"I think we're gonna have some problems," said Jones with a sigh. "I'll call the station."

Alexei Khrenkov looked ashen and wasn't breathing. His pupils had shrunk to pinpoints.

"It looks like he had a stroke," said the hotel doctor, getting to his feet. "It immediately paralyzes the nervous system and shuts off vital functions."

Malko said nothing. This was no stroke, he knew. Khrenkov had been poisoned under his very eyes, killed by a powerful drug in the passport he'd been given. Malko now understood why it had been sealed in a plastic pouch. Contact with air probably turned the poison into a deadly gas.

A hotel staffer discreetly covered the body with a blanket to shield it from guests' eyes. A public killing wasn't really the Imperial's style.

Malko noticed Khrenkov's red passport on the floor and used a tablecloth to wrap and retrieve it. Feeling bitter and angry, he phoned the American embassy.

The Russians had succeeded despite all of his precautions. They had managed to kill Khrenkov before he could deliver the list of swallows.

Police officers in green uniforms were entering the hotel lobby.

"Did you know the dead man, sir?" one asked Malko.

"Yes. He was a Russian defector, and they killed him."

Seeing the officer's bafflement, he went on:

"You will get the details from the *Stadtpolizei*. And someone from the Central Intelligence Agency is on his way over."

"And do you know the two Americans who shot a man near here?"

"Yes, I do. They are CIA agents, and they were on duty. I'm sorry, but I have to leave you now."

Lynn Marsh was probably worried that Khrenkov hadn't returned. Malko felt he ought to be the person to tell her what happened.

When she opened the door to the suite, Malko felt a pang. Wearing an orange dressing gown, she looked beautiful, even without makeup.

"Where's Alexei?" she asked. "Did he get his passport?"

When Malko remained silent, the young woman turned pale.

"My God, did something happen?"

"Yes," he said simply.

He waited until Lynn was seated on the yellow sofa before describing Khrenkov's death.

"They killed him," he said. "Right before my eyes. I feel terribly guilty."

She heard him out. Then she looked straight at him, her eyes empty, her face haggard.

"I hate you," she said dully. "All this happened because of you. Without you, Alexei would still be alive."

"I'm not so sure about that," he said. "Zhanna Khrenkov wanted to kill you. None of this is anyone's fault. It's a Greek tragedy, and it was written the moment Alexei fell in love with you."

Lynn didn't answer, absorbing what Malko had just said. Then she turned to ask, her eyes full of tears:

"What's to become of me?"

A good question.

"I suppose you can go back to London," he said. "We'll ask MI5 to protect you."

She shook her head.

"I don't want to go back to England. Not right away, at least. I'm too scared."

"Give it some thought," he suggested. "Gwyneth will guard you here in the meantime."

Matt Hopkins, the Vienna CIA station chief, was chairing the meeting with Richard Spicer and Malko. Three hours had passed since Khrenkov was taken to the morgue. Assisted by the American consul general, Chris Jones and Milton Brabeck were being questioned by the Austrian police.

"Did the police tell you anything about the killer?" Malko asked Hopkins.

"Not much, unfortunately. He wasn't carrying any ID. But he was wearing two pairs of latex gloves under his leather ones."

"Why?"

"The forensic officers think Khrenkov was killed with a sarin-like organophosphorus compound. They block neurotransmission, which leads to shrinking of the pupils and paralysis of the nervous system. At first blush, the victim appears to have died of a cerebral embolism."

Richard Spicer spoke up.

"The Russians have always liked using poison. Ever since the end of the war, their scientists have been working on compounds that kill by inhalation. They're incredibly toxic. All you need is a few milligrams of poison in solid form. That's what must've been in the passport. When Khrenkov opened it, this started a reaction with the ambient air, and he breathed in the suspended particles. The guy who brought the passport was wearing the extra gloves for protection."

"I told Langley what happened," said Spicer gloomily. "It looks like Khrenkov took his secret to the grave. We don't even know what bank has his network list."

"Not that they'd give it to you," said Hopkins. "I know the Swiss."

He turned to Malko.

"You've done everything you could, Malko. It's time to wind this operation down. As far as our two guys are concerned, we should be able to work things out with the Austrians."

"I hope so," said Malko. "They were just doing their job."

The Russians must be rubbing their hands in glee, he thought bitterly. They would soon reactivate their network.

"What do you plan to do with Lynn Marsh?" Spicer abruptly asked.

That was a question Malko wasn't expecting.

"I have no idea," he admitted. "Why?"

"Langley says we can't be responsible for her. Best thing to do is to send her back to London. After all, she's a British citizen."

Malko remained silent. He knew how cold-blooded the CIA could be. When you'd served your purpose, you were discarded. Aloud he said:

"But she's still in danger. The Russians tried to kill her in London. She's a target too, you know."

"I understand, and that's too bad," said Spicer. "I'll ask the Austrian police to keep an eye out for her."

"Like a sleepy chaperone!" cried Malko. "You know they won't put much effort into it."

Spicer looked away. He clearly wasn't going to lie awake nights worrying about Lynn Marsh's fate. He ostentatiously glanced at his watch and said:

"Well, I have to go talk to the cops. Let's meet again in the morning."

Malko found he had trouble shaking his old friend's hand. With the Americans it was always the same thing, he reflected. When an operation was over, they wound things down, the way they wound things down in Afghanistan after the victory over the Soviets.

And everyone knows how that turned out.

Malko had just passed through the Hotel Imperial's revolving door when he bumped into Alexandra. She was carrying a couple of shopping bags and was heading for the elevator.

"Ah, none too soon!" she said playfully, kissing him lightly on the mouth. "Are you all done with your spooks? I asked Elko to come get us in half an hour. We're invited to a party at the Wittgensteins, and I'll need time to change. You'll see, I bought a dress you're going to like."

In the face of Malko's silence, she asked:

"What's going on? Is there a problem?"

"For Alexei Khrenkov, a pretty serious one."

Unmoved, she listened to his account, then said:

"So what's the problem? We drive back to Liezen, and your little dentist hops a plane for London. Or she stays here. It's her problem. Okay, I'm going to get ready."

Striding imperiously, Alexandra marched to the elevators as a bellman scurried over to carry her bags. Malko waited a moment before taking the elevator in his turn.

Lynn Marsh's face looked ravaged by sorrow. She was wearing a terry-cloth robe and sobbing loudly. Gwyneth Robertson, who opened the door for Malko, whispered before she left:

"She's been drinking a lot of cognac."

A half-full bottle of Delamain stood on a side table.

When they were alone, Malko asked:

"Have you decided what to do?"

"I don't want to go back to London," she managed to say between sobs.

"Staying here is dangerous. The local CIA people can't offer you further protection, and the Austrians don't care. So—"

"What about you?" she asked, interrupting him. "Can't you protect me?"

Malko was silent, seeing his problems multiplying.

"Of course I could," he admitted, "but I'm due to go home later today, to Liezen Castle."

The young woman leaped to her feet, blazing with anger.

"You bastard!" she screeched. "You're ditching me, aren't you? And they're going to kill me."

Malko felt ashamed of himself.

"I'll certainly ask the Austrians to protect you," he promised.

He found Lynn Marsh's eyes locked laser-like on his.

"I don't want to die," she said. "It's up to you to protect me. You certainly did in London. Even slept over at my apartment."

Malko wanted to tell her that there was no Alexandra in London.

Feminine intuition suddenly told her what was happening.

"You're afraid, aren't you? What are you afraid of?"

Awareness growing in her eyes, she crie`d:

"I got it! It's your girlfriend! You're a coward, like all men. You'd rather see me killed than make a scene!"

By now, she was out of control. As Malko remained silent, she took a step closer.

"In that case, I'll give you one good reason to protect me!"

With that, she calmly undid her terry-cloth robe and let it fall. Underneath, she was completely naked.

Malko couldn't help but admire her perfect body, high breasts, flat stomach. A saucy woolly triangle topped her long legs. In heels, she was as tall as he was.

"Fuck me," she said. "I know you've wanted to since our evening at Christie's. That way, you'll have a reason to look after me."

Under the young woman's icy stare, Malko didn't know what to do with himself. He had rarely experienced a situation so embarrassing.

And humiliating.

"Get dressed," he finally said, finding his voice. "I have a duty to protect you, and I'll take you to Liezen. Be ready to go in half an hour."

At the door, he turned around. Lynn had picked up her robe and was walking toward the bedroom, displaying a magnificent back and ass.

Alexei Khrenkov had died too soon.

Dressed in a heavy green blouse and leather pants stuffed into high-heel boots, she looked every inch the gentlewoman farmer.

"So, did you bid your tooth fairy good-bye?"

"Actually, I didn't," said Malko. "She's in mortal danger, and I have to take her to Liezen."

He thought Alexandra would rip his throat out.

"You're joking!" she roared.

"No, I'm not."

"And she's coming in our car?"

Her voice had now become dangerously soft.

"I'm afraid so."

"Then she can ride in the trunk! That's where we put whores!"

Unintentionally stoking the flames, Lynn Marsh emerged

from the elevator just then, looking quite fetching in her white wool suit and black stockings.

"That does it!" snapped Alexandra. "That bitch isn't getting into my car."

She barked an order to the two bellmen, who snatched up her Louis Vuitton suitcases and marched to the revolving door. Malko watched as she climbed into the Jaguar while the bellmen packed the trunk. The car roared off minutes later.

Malko had been driving on the A4 highway toward Liezen for the last twenty minutes. Lynn Marsh was dozing on the passenger seat next to him, done in by cognac and nervous tension. Traffic was heavy, and it looked as if it would take them an hour to get home, though Liezen was only about thirty miles from Vienna.

The castle was in Burgenland, the eastern strip of Austria bordering Hungary, a sunny lowland that produced well-balanced white wines. The first windmills soon appeared. They were getting closer.

After vainly trying to raise Alexandra on her cell, he had lost half an hour renting the Mercedes. Lynn had said nothing.

Malko was furious at himself. He hated when his two lives overlapped, that of the country gentleman—*Seine Hoheit, der Prinz*—and that of the high-level CIA contract operative. But without the Agency's generous paychecks, his castle would be nothing but a ruin.

Liezen Castle was a bottomless pit, and despite the money he had sunk in it, Malko still hadn't managed to completely restore it. Two wings were empty, without working bathrooms and furnished with mismatched castoffs. Yet if you could somehow grind up the castle's old stones and press them, blood would flow out.

Because it was by risking his life for the CIA that Malko was able to maintain his modest but decent lifestyle.

He left the A4 for Route 10, and pulled into the Liezen Castle courtyard a few minutes later. The Jaguar wasn't there. Elko Krisantem, resplendent in a white jacket and bow tie, came down the front steps to meet them.

The Turkish killer-for-hire turned butler was as bent and knotty as an old oak branch and devoted to Malko.

With a smile on his hawk-like face, he opened Lynn Marsh's door.

She stepped out of the Mercedes and gazed at the castle's majestic façade.

"And this belongs to you?"

"Yes, it does," said Malko. To Krisantem, he said:

"Please put Dr. Marsh in the Blue Room. By the way, where is the countess?"

"She went to Kittsee Castle, sir. To the Wittengensteins."

To the party he and Alexandra were supposed to attend together. Seeing Malko's obvious annoyance, the old Turk murmured:

"Your Highness should have given me instructions. The countess wouldn't have left."

Krisantem's view of women's rights was close to the Taliban's. In his eyes, an honest woman should leave her house only twice in her life: the first time to get married, and the second to be buried in the cemetery.

Malko watched as the butler led Lynn Marsh up the stone staircase, then went to the library and poured himself a glass of vodka. He now had a new dilemma. He could still join Alexandra in Kittsee, but he would be coming hat in hand.

He decided it might be smart to sit tight and await developments.

———

Krisantem rapped lightly on the library door.

"I have laid out your tuxedo, Your Highness. And the lady in the Blue Room would like to see you."

"I'm on my way," said Malko.

He would see that Lynn was safely settled, and then drive to Kittsee. In her defiance, Alexandra had gone there much too early; the party wouldn't start until later.

Reaching the first floor, Malko knocked on the door to the room.

"Come in," cried Lynn.

Her voice sounded odd. He opened the door on the room's four-poster bed in the light of the big chandeliers. Glancing around, he realized that the bed was empty and that Lynn had made a good start on a bottle of Steinhäger gin on the coffee table.

As he turned to look for her, she appeared from behind the door—and gave him a jolt of adrenaline. Except for a pair of high heels, the young woman was completely naked. She had freshened her makeup and had a slightly crazed sparkle in her eyes.

Without a word, she wrapped her arms around Malko's neck. Draping herself against him, she pressed her mouth to his, her tongue urgent. Malko understood where the Steinhäger had gone.

"Now fuck me," she said quietly, slurring the words a little.

Lynn relieved Malko of his clothes, then seized and furiously stroked his cock. And it was she who pulled him to the bed, where she fell back, legs apart.

When he entered her, she raised her hips a little to ease him in deeper. Her enjoyment was probably stoked by what was both a reclaiming of power and a victory over another woman.

Now she was moving under him, giving little thrusts with her hips, groaning with pleasure. As Alexandra had guessed, Dr. Lynn Marsh loved to fuck.

Just when he was about to come, she pulled away and turned around, kneeling with her hips raised. It was an unambiguous invitation.

The sight of her firm, rounded rump dismissed Malko's few remaining scruples. He penetrated her in a single thrust, then seized her hips and started pounding away. Gripping the four-poster's linen curtains with both hands, Lynn suffered his assault with delight.

When Malko came deep inside her, he couldn't help but remember how devastated she'd looked when he announced the death of her lover, Alexei Khrenkov.

La donna è mobile . . .

In the darkness, Malko looked at the glowing hands on his Breitling. It was ten past nine. He still had time to make it to Kittsee.

As if reading his mind, Lynn rolled onto her side and pressed against him.

"Make love to me again! I need to forget all those horrors."

Unable to stir, Malko said nothing.

"I don't want you to leave," she continued. "I'm too frightened."

If only he could wave a magic wand, thought Malko, and make a copy of himself.

Like a scented serpent, Lynn's head slid down Malko's belly, where she gently took his resting cock in her mouth. She moved her head only very slightly, but Malko could feel a new erection rising. Driving to Kittsee was now out of the question.

Just then, Lynn raised her head from his lap and looked up at him.

"You did well to bring me here," she said quietly. "I may have a nice surprise for you."

Malko abruptly lost all interest in sex, a fact that Lynn Marsh immediately noticed.

"You really are a coldhearted bastard!" she cried, kneeling on the bed. "Does it always take a twisted spy story to give you a hard-on?"

She was glowering at him, almost with contempt. The Steinhäger had clearly had its effect.

"Three people have already died in this business, Lynn," he said. "Including Alexei, the man you loved."

"You know, I'm not sure I really was in love with him. I was bored when we met, and he excited me, opened up a world I didn't know. But as a lover, he was a bear."

She rolled onto her back, smiling to herself.

"There's something you aren't telling me," said Malko after a moment. "What is it?"

She smiled more broadly.

"Alexei wasn't as naïve as he appeared," she said. "He didn't trust the Russians. So he gave me the key and access code to his safety-deposit box, in case something happened to him. It's at Crédit Suisse, on rue du Rhône."

Malko needed a moment to absorb this.

"What do you plan to do about it?" he asked carefully.

Lynn looked at him ironically.

"If you'd dumped me at the Imperial, you would never have known about it. I wouldn't have said anything, just gone on with my life. Now, things are different."

"Are you prepared to give me access to those documents?"

"Yes."

Malko felt as if he had sprouted wings and was touching the sky.

"All right!" he said. "We're leaving for Geneva tomorrow."

"Let's not go too early," she said with a sigh. "I want the fun and games to last a little longer."

Without waiting for Malko's response, she bent her head to resume her interrupted fellatio.

After an uneventful flight, the Falcon 2000 came in for a smooth landing at Geneva Airport. Glancing out the window, Malko saw a black limousine flying an American flag, followed by two black minibuses with tinted windows. The CIA agents he assumed were inside would supplement the four case officers who had flown with him and Lynn Marsh from Vienna. The Agency wasn't taking any chances this time.

Chris Jones and Milton Brabeck weren't along, however. They'd been kicked out of Austria and had returned to the United States.

The Falcon left the main runway and rolled to a stop on a strip far from the main terminal, where it was met by the three embassy vehicles, led by a Swiss police car. As Malko stepped down the ladder, the first person he saw was Richard Spicer. The London station chief shook his hand warmly.

"Well done!" he said.

Their group left the terminal by an exit off-limits to the public and headed downtown. They were driving along the lake when Spicer turned to Malko and said:

"We've alerted the bank. They better not make a fuss."

The bank made no fuss at all, and the sealed documents about the Russian spy ring were soon in a CIA safe at the American embassy. Not long afterward, Malko, Lynn, and Spicer were eating Peking duck at the Tsé Yang, the Hotel Kempinski's Chinese restaurant.

Now that she had helped produce the envelope, Lynn's mind seemed elsewhere.

"What would you like to do now, Dr. Marsh?" asked Spicer.

"I've decided I want to go home to London after all. The sooner the better. And never think of any of this again."

"That's easy enough. You can fly back with me in the Falcon. We're leaving at four."

Malko spoke up.

"Lynn, there's a chance the Russians are going to seek revenge. Wouldn't you rather go somewhere other than London?"

"We'll provide Dr. Marsh protection for as long as it takes," said Spicer. "Besides, our friend Sir William has warned the Russians that touching a hair on her head would be seen as an act of war against Great Britain. The Russians aren't crazy. They'll go to any length to stop something from happening, but not to take revenge."

"From your lips to God's ear," said Malko dubiously.

Lunch was over. Taking no chances, they rode an elevator down to the underground garage, where they went their separate ways. Without meeting his eye, Lynn gave Malko a long handshake, then got into the embassy Cadillac.

The London station chief was practically glowing.

"You can go back to Austria with a light heart!" he said. "The ball's in our court now. But I think the Agency is going to call on you again. Very soon, in fact."

"To do what?"

"You'll see, it's a surprise. A good one."

Spicer climbed into the Cadillac in turn, and Malko took the elevator back up. There was a flight for Vienna at 6:50.

Informed of Lynn Marsh's stay at Liezen Castle by Krisantem, Alexandra had chosen to sleep elsewhere.

Malko had been reading the *Washington Post* and following the dismantling of the Khrenkov network for the last week. On June 27, 2010, the FBI arrested ten of the spies in simultaneous raids.

In Washington, the Russian ambassador swore to high heaven that it was all an FBI plot, that none of the Russian secret services and no SVR officer was involved. Which was perfectly true, since the network had been completely independent of the D.C. and New York *rezidenturas*.

No new arrests had been made in the last few days, and the spy story was fading from the front page.

Just then, Alexandra entered the library. She was dressed like a slutty winemaker, wearing pants so tight that the grapes would practically pick themselves.

"I've invited the Von Thyssens for dinner," she announced. "Better warn Ilse." Malko's old cook could work wonders, but at her age she needed some advance notice.

Malko stood to kiss his fiancée, and she kissed him back. They hadn't mentioned Lynn Marsh again. When Malko got back from Geneva, Alexandra greeted him as if nothing had happened. Krisantem alerted her that the English guest had departed, and she returned to the castle as soon as Malko left for Geneva.

In fairness, he hadn't asked her any questions about her prolonged stay at Kittsee Castle, either.

All was for the best in the best of all possible worlds.

His encrypted BlackBerry began to beep. It was Richard Spicer.

"You have a meeting tomorrow morning at Boltzmanngasse," he said.

"What's it about?"

"Crowning your success."

Two black Mercedes with diplomatic plates were parked in front of the Red Cross's Vienna offices when the U.S. embassy Cadillac pulled up across the street.

Malko stepped out, accompanied by the American ambassador and his Russian interpreter.

A cheerful Viennese woman led them to a conference room normally reserved for inter-community meetings, its walls decorated with posters touting the Red Cross's charitable work.

Three men who looked like clones were already in the room, and they stood as one when the new arrivals entered. With them was an interpreter, who addressed the American ambassador in English.

"I would like to introduce Vice Minister Vasily Yakushin," he said, gesturing toward the man in the middle. "He and his two deputies came from Moscow this morning in order to resolve the difficulties that exist between the American government and ours. President Medvedev has given Gospodin Yakushin full authority to negotiate an agreement."

The American ambassador's answer was translated into Russian.

"We're happy to be meeting you in this neutral space. I would like to introduce Mr. Malko Linge, whom the American government has designated to represent us in these negotiations. He also has been granted full authority to reach an agreement. Mr. Linge speaks Russian fluently, which will help avoid misunderstandings. We'll withdraw so you can begin the discussions."

The ambassador and his interpreter left the hall. The Russian interpreter stayed just long enough to offer everyone tea, and withdrew in turn. This left the three Russians on one side, and Malko and a stenographer on the other.

Malko spoke first.

"Gospoda, I'm sure you know that the Federal Bureau of Investigation has recently arrested ten people in various American states engaged in espionage for Russia. They were part of a network that the FBI broke up with the help of outside information.

"In view of the good relations between Russia and the United States, the American government doesn't want to see this situation deteriorate. I have therefore been charged with resolving the problem."

None of the Russians seemed to find unusual the fact that an Austrian citizen should be speaking in the name of the U.S. government. They were well aware of Malko's role in uncovering the *lastochkas* network.

It was Vice Minister Yakushin's turn to speak.

"Our government is in no way responsible for the actions of these people," he said primly. "This so-called network is obviously a plot hatched by rogue members of the American espionage establishment to damage the friendship between our two countries."

Nice example of double-talk, thought Malko to himself.

Ignoring the Russian official's statement, he said:

"I've been asked to tell you some steps that the White House is considering. These people, who are currently in jail, would normally be charged with espionage and brought to trial in United States federal court. If found guilty, they could be sentenced to many decades in prison. Needless to say, the media would broadcast any revelations that came out during such trials. The FBI investigation has produced irrefutable evidence that the leaders of the network were in Moscow. In other words, this was a state-sponsored operation.

"Obviously, this would lead to a deterioration in relations between the United States and Russia."

The three Russians seemed to have been turned to pillars of salt.

Malko paused to take a sip of tea before continuing.

"However, another solution is possible, which would do much less harm to our relationship. The individuals involved would be charged with acting as unregistered agents of a foreign power."

One of the Russians was feverishly taking notes. Malko gave him time to catch up, then concluded:

"As a criminal matter, this is a much less serious charge than espionage, and would be followed by the defendants' expulsion from the United States."

In other words, Russia would get its spies back.

Despite this apparently conciliatory offer, the Russians didn't crack a smile. Seeing that Malko was finished, Yakushin spoke again, in a carefully neutral tone.

"We support the second approach, of course. When could it be put into effect?"

Malko found his seeming naïveté charming. He smiled slightly when one of Yakushin's deputies chimed in.

"So these people would be allowed to fly home to Russia?"

Malko shook his head.

"Not directly, no. They would travel through Vienna first, here in Austria. The Austrian government has agreed to allow them short-term transits through the airport without visas."

The Russian official pretended not to understand.

"Why the stopover?"

"To allow for an exchange," said Malko.

"What kind of exchange?" asked the vice minister sharply.

Malko handed a sheet of paper to the stenographer, who placed it in front of the Russians, and continued:

"For humanitarian reasons, the American government wants to receive four Russian citizens who are currently serving long prison terms for espionage on behalf of the Western powers.

"In the framework of an agreement, these four people would be deported from Russia and brought to Vienna. From here, they could leave for any destination they chose."

The three Russian officials gathered around to read Malko's note. Their response was quick in coming.

"This is impossible!" barked Yakushin. "These individuals are criminals, convicted and sentenced under Russian law."

Malko remained impassive.

"You have the right to refuse the offer," he said. "The American government has set itself a deadline of forty-eight hours before bringing charges in federal court. If you decide to change your position, it would be advisable to alert the American embassy so we can schedule another meeting."

Malko stood up, gestured politely to the three Russians, and headed for the door, followed by the stenographer.

His blood boiling, Rem Tolkachev studied the account of the Vienna meeting with disgust. He regretted that the Khrenkovs had died so quickly. They deserved to rot in the gulag for years.

His prized *lastochkas* network was collapsing, a debacle

sparked by one woman's blind jealousy and a wildly unlikely set of circumstances. He snatched up the red telephone that connected him to the president's office. An assistant answered immediately. The spymaster said:

"I would like to discuss a problem with President Medvedev before the end of the day."

The Red Cross conference room was unchanged, as were the protagonists. Malko had cautiously decided to spend the night at the Hotel Sacher instead of returning to Liezen. That turned out to be wise. The American embassy phoned at nine in the morning to say that another meeting had been scheduled with the Russian delegation for noon, which was two p.m. Moscow time.

Malko entered the room with the stenographer and smiled at Yakushin. The smile was not returned. Instead, the Russian got straight to business.

"For humanitarian reasons, President Medvedev has decided to pardon the following three defendants currently in prison: Igor Sutyagin, sentenced in 2004 to fifteen years; Alexander Zaporozhsky, an SVR colonel, convicted of treason and sentenced to eighteen years; and Sergei Skripal, a colonel expelled from the GRU, later tried for espionage and sentenced in 2006 to thirteen years."

Yakushin stopped talking while the American stenographer noted the information, then went on.

"These three individuals will be expelled from Russia and can travel to any country they like."

"When?" asked Malko.

"When the people arrested by the FBI are expelled from the United States."

Malko waited for a moment, then said:

"There were four names on the list I gave you. The fourth person is Gennady Vasilenko. He was arrested in 2006 and, according to his family, is serving fourteen years in prison."

For the first time, Yakushin lost some of his calm demeanor.

"Gennady Vasilenko is a stain on the honor of the First Directorate!" he cried. "He was already identified as a spy in 1982 and imprisoned at Lefortovo. He had been working for the CIA for several years, but he was freed for lack of a confession. The FSB caught him red-handed spying again in 2004. The man deserves to die."

Yakushin's anger was genuine.

Malko gave the storm time to pass, then carefully gathered the papers in front of him.

"I was given very precise instructions," he said. "The agreement I proposed can only be completed with the delivery of all four of the prisoners named. I should remind you that the United States deadline expires tomorrow."

Malko stood up.

"*Dasvidanya.*"

He left the conference hall in dead silence. Glancing at his watch, he saw that he had time to join Alexandra for a light lunch at the Sacher's Rote Bar.

The call came through at 2:34 p.m., just as he was about to go upstairs for an erotic nap with Alexandra. "Your damn spooks never give us a moment's peace!" she snapped, frowning in annoyance.

Yakushin's face was so contorted, he looked like a bulldog. He barely gave Malko time to sit down before brusquely saying:

"President Medvedev has agreed to pardon Gennady Vasilenko."

From his scowl, Yakushin apparently viewed the Russian leader as practically a traitor to the nation.

Malko nodded.

"That's a decision that does him great credit," he said smoothly. "In that case no further obstacles remain to putting our accord into effect."

"President Medvedev will sign the pardons this evening," said Yakushin shortly. "We can have a plane here from Moscow tomorrow."

"That's perfect," said Malko. "I will see to the arrangements for transferring your citizens. The two planes should arrive at roughly the same time. The flight to Vienna is longer from the United States."

Yakushin was already on his feet.

"Just let our embassy know. Someone is always on duty."

Vienna International Airport lay baking in the July sun, and heat rose shimmering from the American ambassador's Cadillac. It was parked next to a Boeing 777 from New York about half a mile from the main terminal. The area had been cordoned off by the Austrian police.

The Boeing's door was open and a stairway was in place, but no one had yet come out.

"I certainly hope they show up!" said Malko with a sigh.

He hadn't seen his Russian counterparts since the second meeting. The final details of the accord had been settled on the telephone.

A yellow Volkswagen from the control tower drove over to them. An airport employee stepped out and said:

"The flight from Moscow is on final approach. It will land in a quarter of an hour."

Above the main runway, a white twin jet came into view, bearing a red-and-blue stripe and the name of a Russian charter company.

It was still taxiing when the Russian ambassador's Mercedes appeared. Vice Minister Vasily Yakushin and his two clones stepped out. Malko went over to meet them. The men did not shake hands.

The Russian twin jet rolled closer, and the howl of its engines soon made it impossible to speak. When they finally fell silent, the plane's portside door opened, and the airport ground crew rolled a ladder over.

Yakushin turned to Malko and said:

"*Davai!*"

Malko spoke some instructions into his cell phone. Everything had been programmed in advance, second by second.

It was like in the days of the Cold War when spies were traded across the Glienicke Bridge. There too, every step of the ceremony was carefully orchestrated.

In a few moments, three women emerged from the Boeing. They walked down the ladder and went to stand in a cordoned-off area between the two planes.

Twenty seconds later, a man emerged from the Russian twin jet and went to stand in the cordoned square.

And so the exchange went, three for one, until they were down to the fourth and last passenger aboard the Russian plane. A tall man in a broad-brim fedora appeared, and he stepped down the ladder onto the tarmac.

Yakushin turned to Malko and said, somewhat aggressively:

"*Harasho?* Are we finished?"

Malko looked at him coolly and said:

"*Nyet*, Gospodin Yakushin."

———

The Russian official started, his face reddening.

"What's the matter?" he snapped. "We have held up our end of the agreement."

Malko pointed to the final passenger to emerge, the tall man in the hat.

"That isn't Gennady Vasilenko."

For a moment, he thought the Russian was going to choke.

"How can you say that?" he practically shouted.

"Because I know him."

Which was true. Malko had secretly met with Vasilenko on one of his assignments in Moscow. That was one reason the CIA had chosen him to oversee the spy swap.

A heavy silence followed, which Malko eventually broke.

"I don't imagine you're foolish enough to have left Vasilenko back in Moscow. If he doesn't come out of that plane in three minutes, the whole deal is off."

After a long pause, Yakushin waddled toward the Russian jet with the grace of an angry elephant and climbed the ladder. Moments later he reappeared in the company of a tall, hatless man who shouted in Russian to the phony Vasilenko in the fedora. The latter tore off his hat and threw it to the ground before striding back to the plane.

The deported Russian spies soon followed him up the ladder into the twin jet.

In ten minutes everything was concluded, and the two planes' doors closed. Malko watched as the Boeing's jets started up.

It gave him some satisfaction to know that the victims of the *lastochkas* affair hadn't died in vain. He had managed to free four people from Russian prisons, where they would certainly have perished.

At peace, he walked back toward the ambassador's limousine. Yakushin had already gotten into the Russian car, stoking his rage.

Several months later, Malko watched the snowflakes whirling against the bedroom windows. Alexandra was still asleep after a very late night and some love games that had left them both exhausted.

He reached for his beeping cell phone. It displayed a British number, and he took the call.

"Malko?"

It was Richard Spicer.

"Hello, Richard! What's the good word?"

The CIA station chief paused before answering.

"The word's not good at all, Malko. Dr. Lynn Marsh was just found drowned in the Thames close to her home. It seems she slipped and fell while jogging along the river."

About the Translator

William Rodarmor (1942–) is a French literary translator of some forty books, including four Malko Linge thrillers for Vintage: *The Madmen of Benghazi, Chaos in Kabul, Revenge of the Kremlin*, and *Lord of the Swallows*. Now retired from a career as a magazine writer and editor, Rodarmor has won the Lewis Galantière Award from the American Translators Association and worked as a contract interpreter for the U.S. State Department.

REVENGE OF THE KREMLIN

In this riveting, tightly plotted tale of espionage, Malko Linge investigates the suspicious death of a Russian oligarch in London. Boris Berezovsky is living in exile in London to avoid the wrath of Vladimir Putin. One morning, the unlucky oligarch is found dead in his bathroom, an apparent suicide. Their suspicions aroused, MI5 opens an investigation—but Prime Minister David Cameron orders the case closed. Alarmed at the renewal of Russian Cold War tricks and Moscow's increasingly close ties to London, the CIA dispatches Malko Linge to investigate Berezovsky's death and the British cover-up. With help from an alluring former CIA handler, Malko dives into the search for hard evidence of the Kremlin's involvement in the affair—putting himself directly in the crosshairs of the world's most efficient assassins.

Thriller

CHAOS IN KABUL

As U.S. troops prepare to withdraw from Afghanistan, and the Taliban is poised to take over, the CIA calls upon the Austrian aristocrat Malko Linge to execute a dangerous and delicate plan to restore stability to the region. On the ground in Kabul, Malko reconnects with an old flame and hires a South African mercenary to assist with his mission. But Malko doesn't know whom he can trust. His every move is monitored by President Karzai's entourage, Taliban leaders, a seductive American journalist—and a renegade within the CIA itself. Before he can pull off his plan, Malko is kidnapped and nearly killed. When he finally manages to escape, he finds himself alone and running for his life in a hostile city.

Thriller

The Madmen of Benghazi is a gripping, racy, ripped-from-the-headlines espionage thriller set in volatile post-Qaddafi Libya. Its hero, Malko Linge, spends his time freelancing for the CIA in order to support his playboy lifestyle. When terrorists try to shoot down a plane carrying Libyan prince Ibrahim al-Senussi, it is clear that someone wants him dead. But the CIA has its own plot for the prince: Now that Qaddafi has been overthrown, al-Senussi is their best bet to set up a constitutional monarchy and stem the Islamist tide in Libya. The CIA, which needs Malko as much as he needs them, sends the Austrian aristocrat to Cairo to learn more about al-Senussi's plans by seducing his companion, a ravishing British model. This mission is enormously appealing, but also proves enormously dangerous, as the same madman of God who is trying to kill al-Senussi also takes aim at Malko.

Thriller

FORTHCOMING FROM
VINTAGE CRIME/BLACK LIZARD

Surface to Air: A Malko Linge Novel
June 2016

VINTAGE CRIME/BLACK LIZARD
Available wherever books are sold.
www.weeklylizard.com